Nietzsche's Horse

Patrick Wallace Hazzard

An Intellect Publishing Book

www.IntellectPublishing.com

Copyright ©2023 Patrick Wallace Hazzard

ISBN: 978-1-954693-75-3

First Edition: March 2023

FV-12

Inquiries to: info@IntellectPublishing.com

Dedicated to Martin Greenberg, MD.

Patrick Wallace Hazzard

Nietzsche's Horse

1

If I can say lately that I've been standing on my own two feet, then today was a day for looking down and finding nothing under them.

I was sitting by myself at a table on the top floor of the college library when two girl students and a boy sat down at the table next to mine. They opened their backpacks, and after shuffling their stuff around and murmuring to each other, they settled down and began reading.

When several minutes had passed, one of the girls whispered: "Look at him."

My ears pricked up, and then she said: "Look at him. Look at his body."

Oh, no! They're talking about me! If I look up, I'll catch them staring at my body!

I didn't look up.

"Look at his body," the girl whispered again. "What does it look like?"

There was another silence, and then the other two spoke at the same time.

"A girl," the boy said.

"A dancer," said the second girl.

"Yeah, a dancer," the first girl said, ignoring the boy's remark. "See all those muscles in his legs? Dancing really builds them up!"

"Yeah, cool!" the second girl agreed. "I wish mine looked that good in tights!"

I glanced over and saw that the first girl held an open book up toward her friends, showing them a photo of a man in black tights, frozen midair in a flying leap.

What a relief! It wasn't me after all!

But why did I think it was?

What if something like this happens to me when I'm teaching my first freshman writing class? Let's just say I'm standing in front of the class, describing the way the course will go, and two students in the back row lean toward each other, start to whisper, and then break into giggles!

Would I get the familiar neck-crawling chill of fear that grabbed me today? Would some voice in my head try to convince me the students were whispering about ME?

Yes! Yes! It would!

So much for my plans to teach for a living while I launch a writing career. I'd dissolve in front of a class at the first hint of ridicule!

Dissolve? Really, Wallace? Dissolve?

Well, maybe not dissolve, but freeze and not be able to speak another word.

So, where does that leave me? I've tried other day jobs that didn't require public speaking. For example, house carpentry. But ten hours a day on my feet, swinging a hammer in the hot sun or cold wind, didn't leave time or energy for writing.

I apprenticed as a cabinet maker in a friend's shop, and I even tried running my own shop for three years, being my own boss and writing in my "spare time."

Spare time? What a joke! What spare time? Hard experience taught me what any start-up business owner soon learns about spare time. There's none of that to spare!

So, today was a day for me to imagine dead ends:

I can't teach freshman writing because of a terminal case of stage fright.

I've wasted years proving to myself that I can't work in the skilled trades and still have time and energy enough to write.

What does that leave? Plenty, but today all I could see were the dead ends, and behind them, the specter of the funny farm!

How far have I come in the past twelve years? These were the same dead-end daymares that I dreamed over and over again during the year I spent at the University of Basel.

On days like today, nothing seems to have happened since — nothing I've done seems real. I feel like a neurotic spider, spinning round and round in my own head, wrapping myself in my own tight web.

"Aber, Wallace!" I can hear Kaspar saying to me. *"Du bist gar nicht neurotisch!"* You're not neurotic, at all!

Like me, Kaspar was a student at the university, but he studied medicine, and his upbeat diagnosis carried significant weight with me. So it helped to lift some of the weight I had loaded on my own shoulders.

Kaspar was the best friend I made that year in Switzerland, and the day he spoke those reassuring words, we sat in his small attic flat in the heart of the Old Town of Basel. I had just finished unloading all my doubts and fears on him, as well as my self-diagnosis of neurosis.

To strengthen his case, he pulled his medical dictionary from a small, wall-hung bookcase and opened it to the entry for neurosis. After reading aloud the bizarre symptoms, he looked up at me and said:

"Du hast keines dieser Symptome, oder?" You don't have any of these symptoms, do you?

"Nein, wahrscheinlich nicht," I said. No, apparently not.

In truth, I hadn't understood very many of the scientific German and Latin terms Kaspar read from the dictionary definition, so I just let it pass. But I thought, *Just give me time, and I'll work a few of them up.*

And a few days later, something happened at the university that convinced me my feelings of oddness were not just in my mind. I was becoming odd on the outside, too.

I was walking down a hallway between classes, dreaming my life into dead ends, when I noticed two guys standing to one side, talking to each other.

They looked Swiss-German, but they dressed very French, very stylish and trim. One wore a crew-neck sweater with his shirt collar out and the sleeves of the sweater and shirt pushed up to his elbows. The other wore gold, wire-framed glasses, with his sweater draped over his shoulders and the sleeves crossed over his chest.

As I drew near them, they turned and looked at me. I glanced away and kept walking. My legs felt stiff and awkward, so I straightened up and tried to walk with a manly, tough swing to my arms.

When I reached the turn in the corridor, I looked back and saw the guy with the glasses walking along with his shoulders back, mocking my stiff stride, while the other guy laughed at his pantomime.

A cold, prickly feeling crawled up my shoulders and neck.

What should I do? Go back and ask them, *What the Hell?* Tear off their silly French sweaters? Knock the prissy, round glasses to the floor and grind them under my heel?

Yes! Yes! All that and more!

But that's not what I did, except a thousand times in my head since. Instead, I faked a don't-give-a-damn smile, turned the corner, and walked on down the corridor and out the doors to the street, blinking back tears of rage at what was happening to poor, poor me.

And I set up one more roadblock in my dead-end life.

What would I do if something like that happened to me now? Well, even if I sometimes think I haven't changed in twelve years, I have to admit I wouldn't run off and join the Marines again and ship out to Vietnam for a year. In fact, something like that did happen to me recently, but I'm still here.

It was just after sunrise, and I was walking on the cliff above the ocean, on my way down to run on the beach. The path led beside the railroad tracks and then crossed them and took a deep dive down the face of the cliff.

That morning, four teenage surfers stood on the cliff, watching the waves roll in below. As I neared them, they turned and crossed the tracks and then walked single file across a plank over the storm drain between the tracks and the street.

Before the first surfer reached the other side, the one behind him started jumping on the plank, trying to bounce him off.

Each surfer followed suit, trying to bounce the surfer ahead of him off the plank. When the last surfer reached the other side, he cupped his hands around his mouth and made a loud cat call:

"EEE-gaah!"

When the others laughed, he shouted again:

"EEE-gaah!"

The second shout jogged my memory. Some time after midnight, that same shout had waked me, carried from the cliff to my cabin on an onshore breeze, followed by the sound of muffled laughter.

The surfers stopped by a yellow crew-cab pickup with four surfboards in a rack on top. They pulled out their wetsuits from the cab and began pulling them on, laughing and horsing around with each other the whole time.

I looked at them and thought:

Why don't you let the world sleep? Why fill it with your pointless noise?

Eegah-boy saw me frowning at them, and he frowned right back. Then he stood still and quiet for a moment and growled out in a loud, deep voice:

"*Grand*-daddy!"

Then louder:

"*Grand*-daddy! *Great*-granddaddy!"

I ignored him while I crossed the tracks and walked to the drop off. Just before I stepped over the edge, eegah-boy bellowed "*Granddaddy!*" again with such force, I snapped around and glared at him.

The surfers broke up laughing and piled into the truck, and the driver cranked up the engine and laid rubber up to the corner, where he turned south and screeched out of sight.

I climbed down the trail with my anger still pumping through me. As soon as I hit the sand, I broke into a run, hoping to run the anger out.

But while I ran, eegah-boy's cries kept coming back, along with thoughts about what I *should* have done, *should* have said.

What to do? What lesson did Basel teach me? To go further than he was going? Mock his mocking call? Shoot him the bird? Throw rocks at their pickup? Challenge them to a long-distance run?

No, and that final idea sounded silly, even to me. In fact, the whole thing had taken over my thoughts. It was ruining my run. I had to get it out of my head.

But I couldn't.

Finally, at the end of my run, as I climbed the trail back up the cliff, an idea came to me that might have fit, and that was simply to shout back:

"What, Grandson? What?"

But even that seemed silly and pointless. Not only that, but I could see how absurd it was to waste so much time and energy rehashing the episode, just like the years I wasted thinking about what I should have done to my tormentors in the hallway of the University of Basel.

Instead of circling round and round for years over these episodes in this effort to train myself to make instant, cutting retorts to harassment, why not put my energy into training myself to disengage from the effort?

Putting it simpler, whenever memories like this popped up in my mind, why not just let them come and go, and not do anything about them at all?

Yes! Just let them come and go. So damned simple, but so damned hard!

Then, tonight, when I gave my mind a rest from writing this, I happened to read an article about drunk driving, and one scene got me thinking again about the weird feeling of the earth being cut away from under my feet. It described a head-on collision caused by a drunk driver, who himself died in the tangled wreckage, calling out:

"Mama! Mama!"

And that chilling scene brought back a strong memory of a movie I saw as a boy, *Battleground*. It told the World War II story of the 101st Airborne Division fighting in the Battle of the Ardennes Forest, better known as the Battle of the Bulge.

My father's infantry division, the 84th, had fought in that same battle, from its beginning to its end, and then they fought on, almost without letup, all the way to the Elbe River, where they met up with the lead units of the Russian Army.

Six years after that historic meetup, my father sat between me and my brother in the Trio Theater in Zachary, Louisiana, living through scenes like the ones he had first lived through during that winter of 1944.

My mother hadn't joined us that night because it was a Wednesday, the night for choir practice at our church, where my mother sang in the choir.

And once the action of the movie drew me in, I never gave my mother's absence a moment's thought. One of the characters in the movie especially got my attention, a tall, skinny Southerner named Abner, who spoke with a twangy, nasal accent. When Abner first appeared, he complained he was the only soldier in his squad who hadn't been issued galoshes. These were the thin rubber overshoes that soldiers were issued to strap on over their combat boots to keep their socks and feet dry and warm.

8

Without galoshes, Abner's boots and socks stayed wet and cold from daily soaking in the mud and snow, so Abner kept up his complaining search for galoshes.

Abner pronounced galoshes as go-loshes, with the accent on go, and that made me and my brother laugh. Then, one day, Abner finally got a pair, and he put them on and wore them every day; but strangely enough, he always pulled them off before he slept and placed them outside his foxhole.

The next morning very early, German soldiers in white snow suits sneaked up on Abner's platoon while they still slept, and the first warning for Abner came from the blast of hand grenades, joined by the crackling of rifle fire and the rising roar of machine guns.

Abner reared up in his foxhole and lunged for his galoshes, but just as he grabbed them, tiny spurts of snow shot up first to his left and then his right, marking the path of machine gun bullets that had, alas, crossed Abner.

He slumped face down, body rigid halfway out of the foxhole. His arms remained stretched straight out, his hands still gripping the galoshes. Then he began a slow slide back into his foxhole, dragging the galoshes back with him through the snow.

In the roar of the gunfire, the screen focused on the dark empty mouth of Abner's foxhole, blurring the images of the trees behind Abner, along with the mist and falling snowflakes and rising smoke of the firefight.

Then, for one moment, the gunfire let up, and in the stillness, Abner's voice rose from the hole with the quivering tone of a hurt child:

"Mama... Mama," Abner cried, and then the hole was quiet.

The firing picked up again, joined now by the whistling shriek and muffled crump of artillery rounds exploding beyond their positions.

I leaned up to my father and whispered:

"Is he dead, Daddy? Is he dead?"

He bent his head down and whispered back:

"Yes, honey. He's dead."

My God! Was this what *really* happened in wars?

I had learned by then that people died in wars. They told me that two of my own uncles, both of them pilots, were shot down and killed in World War II.

But this? *This?* Good ole boys like Abner who loved their mothers like I did and said funny things in accents like mine, died alone in frozen muddy holes far away calling out:

Mama? Mama?

I didn't want any part of *that*!

No! What I wanted most right then was my own mother, who was singing away in the bright light and safety of our red brick church.

And right then and there in the movie theater, I decided that I would never let them send me to a war. I could see I just wasn't cut out for it. I knew I wasn't brave enough to go through something like that. And if my fear meant I'd never be the man my father was, that was nothing new to me.

He was a bigger, stronger man than I ever imagined I could even grow up to be. And braver, too. I mean, I had learned that from my very first awareness of how he reacted to suspicious sounds that woke him in the night.

First, he always pulled an all-steel hatchet from its hiding place at the head of his bed. Then he slid out of the bed and slipped quietly through the dark house.

Crouching under my covers in my own bedroom, I couldn't see any of this, but I knew that this big combat vet crept along with a hatchet in one hand, checking the doors and windows, without making any sound that I could hear.

And later on, I learned that he was always a little disappointed because he never found anyone on the other side of the sound that woke him.

So, when I decided at that early age I would never go to a war, the fear of not living up to my father's example didn't loom as large as the fear of being sent to a war to die in a cold, muddy foxhole, calling out, "Mama! Mama!"

A year or so after we watched *Battleground*, the army called my father up again, this time to go fight in Korea. His orders required him to report to an army base near New Orleans for a physical, so we all drove down together, and brought another army vet along who had also received re-up orders.

We set off before dawn, and I remember fog on the road in the swamps between Zachary and New Orleans. Our headlights lit it with a murky yellow glow, creating a dark silhouette of my father in the driver's seat, and the other vet riding shotgun.

My mother rode in the back seat between me and my brother, and I felt safe and cozy snuggling down beside her in the dark.

But I got scared later that day in the sunlight of the army base, parked with my mother and brother beside a large, grassy field where rows and rows of soldiers in white t-shirts and green trousers did push-ups in time to the cadence called by a sergeant in the center of the field, wearing the same uniform with the addition of a Smokey-the-Bear hat.

Back at home the next day, I asked my father if everyone had to serve in the army, which to me at the time meant the same as saying go to a war.

He told me no, that you could become a conscientious objector.

I asked what that meant, and he said you had to believe that war was wrong.

I asked him how you let them know that's what you believed, and he said you had to fill out papers stating your belief, but that wasn't required until you were called up.

At that point in my life, I had not been taught that there was anything wrong about going to war. So I knew I would have to lie when I filled out the papers to become a conscientious objector, because I knew that I would rather lie than have to go to a war.

Fortunately, my father didn't have to go to war again, after all. My mother's bad health prevented it.

And I never had to apply for conscientious objector status, either, because when Vietnam started heating up, I was classified 4-f my freshman year in college when the physical for the Marine Corps NROTC program revealed that I had type-2 diabetes.

So, what was I doing on a December morning seven years later, crawling as fast as I could through the grass of the Que Son River Valley in Vietnam, stinging with pain from the back of my head to the bottom of my ass, with these words revolving in my mind?

I'm ruined! I'm ruined! Oh my God, I'm ruined!

And somewhere to my right, who is calling:

"My god! Help me! Won't somebody please help me?"

The man crying out was a Marine Captain, who had just moments before served as my company commander. Today, I realize he was proving that in moments of extreme pain caused by deadly violence, we don't necessarily call out for our mothers.

But in that moment before death?

I don't know, because the captain didn't die. And later, in the year I spent among the dead and dying, I never found myself near anyone just before they did. And for that, I'm very thankful.

And me? In addition to gathering incomplete data on humans *in extremis*, what was I doing that day? First, I was trying hard to crawl away from the pain. But why was I there in the first place, offering myself up to booby traps on village hillsides?

Because I'm crazy, that's why. If you haven't figured that out by now, it's pretty close to being that simple. For the past twelve years, I've been aware that something inside me can break out and take over. Nothing spectacular, no hallucinations or mad gibbering, just feeling different, odd, and from time to time, enduring a panic attack triggered by stage fright, or ridicule, or by convincing myself that something in the near future will trigger a panic attack.

But I'm getting ahead of myself, or is it behind myself? I mean, I'm circling again, when what I'd like to do is plot a straight course forward. I want to get my life back on track, at least one that meanders in a positive direction instead of this circling around and around.

I'm sick and tired of pissing away all this energy getting nowhere. So, join me while I fly a few more intentional circles–let's call them landing approaches–with the hope of finally coming down from the clouds and landing on solid earth, feet on the ground instead of not so nimbly dancing on the air.

Ready? Okay! Here goes!

* * *

2

Thirteen years ago, during the final week of December, I woke up in a hotel room with a hangover. Not just any hotel room, but one high in the Swiss Alps. It's accessible only by cogwheel railway, and during the winter, the only point of going there is to ski.

Once at the hotel, you can ride ski lifts further up the mountains and ski back down to the hotel, or you can ski down the mountain trails to the towns below– Wengen in one direction, or Grindelwald in the other. And from either, you can take the cogwheel railway back up for another run down and another train ride back up, as many times as light remains in the sky and your legs will still support you.

If you're staying overnight at the hotel, then, after dinner, you can go down to the tavern in the basement for singing and dancing. And if you remain in the tavern long enough and drink enough, you can create a hangover like the one I'm describing.

Not that I recommend it. In fact, for me it created conditions for what you could call my first crack-up. From my perspective, now, I like to call it the first step in my awakening. From what you've read so far, maybe the idea that I'm on a journey of awakening will sound too rosy. After you read further, feel free to pick any word you like in between.

Two other young men shared the room with me—Max and Jurg. Max was the son of my host parents in Basel, and Jurg was one of Max's best friends and a member in their amateur rock band. They had hangovers like mine, created the night before in the tavern, drinking, dancing, singing, and making out later in the hotel lobby with the athletic Swiss girls we befriended during the festivities.

That morning, just the idea of wine brought a shudder of nausea up my throat, and a pang of guilt, too. And more guilt when I pictured where I'd been in the wee hours of that morning, in the lobby of the hotel with Helena, one of those girls. We were standing in one of the dark rooms just off the entrance hall, leaning against the wall, doing our best to achieve the figure of the two-backed, eight-legged, two-headed, human animal, when engaged in the act of mating.

Oh my God! What if her mother had come around the corner just then, looking for her? *Or worse, her father!*

I groaned and turned over in bed and faced the wall.

This brought a laugh from Max.

Jurg cursed instead. *"Gott verdammi, nochmal! Ich habe einen katter!"* God dammit, I've got a hangover!

Just hearing them laugh and crack jokes made me feel a little better.

If they had drunk as much as I had, my behavior wasn't such a hanging matter, was it?

But they hadn't been dry-humping a nice young lady in the front hall, had they?

At that, I felt another stab of guilt, and then another when I remembered missing ski lessons that morning. Ski lessons that Max's father had paid for in advance, along with two weeks of luxury living and frolicking with the rich and fame-avoidant up here in this winter wonderland, a place my own parents could never have afforded.

Instead of giving him his money's worth, though, I had spent the morning unconscious, sleeping off a hangover; and the night before, I'd been fooling around in the hallway with the daughter of a wealthy, influential lawyer with a big practice in Basel, a friend of Max's father, and a fellow distinguished member of the same Rotary Club.

Max and Jurg got up and began to dress and pack quickly. They had to catch the first train after lunch to go back to high school in Basel.

But my holidays from the university weren't over yet, so I was going to stay another week and ski with Max's mother and father and younger sister, who were coming up that afternoon on the late train. I dressed in a hurry and followed Max and Jurg out of the room and down the cold hallway to the door leading outside.

I had been dreading the reflection of sunlight from snow, but the sky was gray with clouds, and we walked through the gray-white pall of snow flurries that gave me a shivery chill. I didn't look forward to skiing that afternoon.

We climbed the front steps of the big hotel and pushed through the heavy glass doors into a small vestibule that served as an airlock against the cold. After stamping the snow off our boots, we pushed through another set of doors that formed the other side of the airlock into the hallway of the hotel.

Max and Jurg left their bags in the lobby where Helena and I had stood against the wall, making out earlier that morning.

My face flushed with shame when I saw the spot, and I was glad I wouldn't have to face her parents this morning, but sad that she was gone.

At lunch, Max and Jurg drank wine with the meal, but I held off. I really felt that drinking now would be drinking because I needed it, which I did; and that was the sure sign of an alcoholic, which, of course I was, but still remained ashamed of owning up to being.

So, by the time for dessert, Max and Jurg were high again, talking and laughing, while I was still subdued with the pain and guilt of my hangover. It was getting too close to train time for them to have dessert, so they said goodbye to me and left me alone at the table.

And then I felt very much alone, for some reason more alone than I had felt in the previous six months I'd spent in Europe. Looking around the room, I saw only wealthy, stylish Europeans. They all belonged there, they were paying their own way, but I'd have never been able to afford this ski trip on my own.

Who was I, anyway? The son of a refinery worker from Baton Rouge, Louisiana.

He was more than that and so was I, but that's the first label-- you are what you do for a living. If one of those wealthy Europeans had asked me what I did or what my father was, I'd have stammered that he was a worker and I was a scholarship boy, and then I would have expected them to drag me out of my chair and throw me out into the snow.

No one did ask, not there anyway, and I doubt they'd have given a damn if they had asked and found out the horrible truth. But I gave a damn, especially without Max and Jurg there to give me something to belong to.

Just when I was feeling like a fake, sitting in this grand hotel setting, my eyes met the eyes of a woman at a table down the room, over the heads of her two young children. I had watched her a lot in the past week. She always sat alone with her children, and I had seen her on the slopes with them, always speaking French. She was

17

beautiful, and she wore well-cut, bright ski clothes. The look she gave me at lunch seemed a coldly appraising one, and I was certain she was thinking to herself, "What's *he* doing here?"

I glanced away nervously and looked out through one of the windows at the snow banked against the building. Then the waiter came with the dessert.

Nothing else I ate that day at lunch is in my memory, but I remember the dessert. It was a scoop of yellow ice cream in a pewter goblet. A thin wafer stuck out of the ice cream, and the goblet stood in a small white saucer. I pulled the wafer out with my left hand and picked up a spoon with my right. For some reason, I thought the French woman might be watching, and that made me even more nervous. I noticed that my hands were trembling.

Without much stomach for it, I spooned up some ice cream and started to raise it to my mouth, but my hand started to tremble even more, and my arm and neck felt stiff and awkward. I put the spoon down on the saucer. My heart was beating faster, and I thought, *What's happening?*

I took a deep breath, and then I picked the spoon back up. But as I raised it, my hand started to shake again, and about halfway up, it felt like some invisible hands were gripping my hand and the back of my neck and holding them apart-- like in a dream when you need to move fast to escape danger, but you can't move at all.

I lowered my arm for a second, and then I made one last effort, lunging down and snapping at the shaking spoon, my head and neck shaking too with an almost rhythmic palsy, like a kid's over a tub of water, bobbing for apples. I dropped the spoon and sat up straight, looking wall-eyed around the room.

Did anyone see? No, no one was looking. My God, what was happening to me? Why couldn't I bring the spoon to my mouth? I had never felt anything like that before. It wasn't just the shakes; it was like some force flowing through me in regular shudders.

Now my heart was pounding. Forget the ice cream, I couldn't try that again. I had to get out of there. I pushed back from the table and stumbled out of the room, keeping my eyes on the floor. Don't let them know, don't let them see, all those grinning, wealthy faces sitting in judgment.

I almost ran back down the hallway toward the lobby. I passed the bar and thought of a drink to calm me down, but that scared me even more. If I drank now, it really meant I was an alky. No, I rushed on down the hallway. Now, today, I want to cup my hands over my mouth and bellow out to that younger me:

"STOP, WALLACE! STOP RUNNING! ONCE YOU GET STARTED, IT'S SO GODAWFUL HARD TO STOP! TURN AROUND, GO BACK! GO TO THE BAR, BELT DOWN A BEER, A WHISKEY, ANYTHING! EAT THE ICE CREAM, FORGET THE EYES OF THE RICH! THEY'RE NOT LOOKING ANYWAY!"

But I don't hear me, of course, I just keep on running. Next, I remember waiting in the lobby for ski school class to begin, staring out the door at the cold, dark day and falling snow, and thinking that the skiing was what I needed, exercise, the cold air, a taste of reality. I certainly didn't want to face the Rosslers without having skied at least half a day.

The teacher of my ski class was a tall, blond Swiss-German named Peter. The class that day was made up of really young Swiss schoolboys. Any one of them could ski better and faster than I could, even at my best, and with the load of dead wine I carried in every muscle, I felt large and clumsy. Their tiny skis and boots and ski clothes, and their quick, frenzied turns and speeding runs made me feel even larger and slower–an ugly American Gulliver among tiny, Swiss Lilliputians.

The only clear memory I have of the run to Grindelwald is of skiing alone down the trail into a ravine. The trail disappeared in a row of fir trees and low bushes, and I could tell it turned to the right because I could hear the shouts of the boys coming up from that direction, muffled by the snow and trees. We were down out of the wind by then, and I was sweating with the effort of trying to keep up. My ski goggles had fogged over, and I had pulled them up on my forehead. My long-john shirt was soaked. But it felt good.

That was what I needed, hard work to sweat out the wine and guilt. I turned down into the ravine and skied through the trees toward the sound of the boys. The ravine opened out onto a gentle slope where everyone stood waiting for me. Just before I reached them, I skied up a small hummock, but I didn't have enough momentum to take me over the top. I slid backward, flailing out behind me with my poles to keep from falling. The boys laughed and I gritted my teeth and cursed them as I poled my way up the rise, but the absurd way I must have looked made me laugh, too.

In Grindelwald, we stacked our skis in a rack outside a small restaurant and went in to have a drink while we waited for the train. Peter and I sat at a small table by a window and ordered hot rum drinks. The waitress brought the rum in glasses that sat in metal frames with cup handles to keep you from burning your fingers on the hot glasses. She also brought a pot of boiling water, a bowl of sugar, and a saucer of lemon slices. Peter spooned sugar and squeezed a slice of lemon into the rum and filled the glass the rest of the way with hot water. I did the same and sipped the hot drink, feeling its warmth move out through my cold body.

When we left the restaurant, it was cold and still outside, and the sun had gone down. There was an orange glow behind the mountains that matched the glow of well-being that I felt from the exercise and the hot rum. Lunch seemed years away and in another world.

That night, though, when I met the Rosslers in the bar for a drink before dinner, I was still worried enough about what happened at lunch to tell them about it. Frau Rossler laughed and said it was just the altitude.

"Did you drink white wine last night?" Herr Rossler asked.

"Yes," I said.

"Well, you see," he said, holding up an index finger, "it was the white wine."

Altitude and white wine, two safe, sane explanations from the real world to still my dark imagination. But not quite still enough. If these were the reasons my hands shook, why had it only happened after Max and Jurg left? Why that? Why did it wait until I was alone? No, there was more to this than white wine and altitude, but for the time being, I let it go.

During the next week I was okay; my hands didn't act up and neither did I. I skied every day, all day, didn't drink after dinner, and I got to bed early. There weren't any more romances that week, either, or early morning love scenes in the lobby. But I must have thought about what had happened at lunch and analyzed why. Maybe not. Maybe that came when things started getting worse, and until then I was content to leave it alone and think of it as an isolated incident. And things did soon get worse.

The only thing I was obligated by contract to do during that fellowship year, other than to attend whatever classes I chose at the university, was to give speeches at Rotary Clubs. The speeches had to be in German, and I would have to give one to any club that invited me. Why? Well, the fellowship was called a Rotary Foundation Fellowship in International Understanding, and the idea behind it went something like this: if you send bright graduate students from every country with Rotary Clubs to other countries with Rotary Clubs, you'll promote international understanding,

That's expecting a lot from graduate students; I mean, most of the ones I've known don't have as a first priority the desire to become goodwill ambassadors for the United States. Still, there was this thing of the speeches. The students had to make speeches about their homelands to Rotary Clubs in the host country, whether they wanted to or not. Can you imagine? I was going to promote the understanding of America in the minds of the presidents and directors of international corporations like Sandoz and Geigy, for example; and raise the consciousness of the editor of the *Basler Nachtrichten*, Peter Durrenmatt, the brother of Friedrich Durrenmatt, the playwright. And I was going to do all this by talking to them for an hour about Baton Rouge, Louisiana, in German. That was the reasoning, and I had signed the contract. Everything has its price, as they always told us.

So, I saw myself faced with having to stand up in front of a crowd of sophisticated European businessmen and talk to them in German that wasn't as good as the English most of them could speak, about a town whose name in French means "red stick". When I put it that way, it no longer surprises me that I began to ask myself the insidious question, "What if my hands shake when I have to give the speeches?"

The first time I remember asking the question, I was typing my speech. It was a Saturday night and I was alone up in my room on the third floor of the Rosslers' house. Max was at his girlfriend's, and the Rosslers had gone out to dinner and the symphony. I must have paused for a minute to read over a phrase, and I pictured the first luncheon in my mind. It was going to be at Olten, a town to the southeast of Basel, a couple of hours by train.

Thinking about the speech was making me feel nervous, and then the thought came, "What if my hands shake when I start to speak, or when I try to eat?" I pictured it, too. First the shaking, my hands trembling on the lectern. I grip it to try to calm them, and I look down at the pages, but my brain refuses to process the meaningless lines of type. I try to speak, to ad lib the words while I look around the room, but my voice is trapped behind the teeth I've clenched to keep my jaw and lips from trembling.

All the club members are casting worried looks at each other during the frozen silence. The silence grows, and my heart pounds into it. I know I have to do something; I just can't stand here! Finally, I can't hold in the shaking any longer, and it explodes up through my chest and neck in a shuddering whiplash that sprawls me face forward onto the lectern. A couple of the members spring up and grab my arms to keep me from falling, and I collapse into their grasp, hiding my sobbing face against a pin-striped shoulder as they lead me out of the room.

That little scene had frozen me at the typewriter in my room at the Rosslers', and I felt my heart pounding in reality. I stood up at the desk, pushing the chair back with my legs, and I took several deep breaths. I had to get out of there; it didn't matter where to, just someplace where there were other people. I stumbled around the room in a circle before my feet found direction and I made it out the door. My knees felt unsteady as I thumped down the carpeted spiral staircase, sliding one hand on the railing to make sure I didn't fall. In the small front hallway, I took my overcoat from a clothes tree and pulled it on as I went out the door.

It helped just to be outside in the cold air, moving, heading somewhere. I walked down to Neuweilerplatz, a junction of five streets where the tram stopped, a few blocks down the hill from the Rosslers'. It was like a small village there, with a post office on one corner, shops, grocers, a drug store, and across the street from the post office, a restaurant on the second floor of a brick building.

Waiting for the tram, I could see the faces of people who sat next to windows in the restaurant. There they were in the warm light, smiling and talking to friends and loved ones, while I stood out alone in the cold. Poor me. Could anyone have it as bad as I did? It was all right for them to have a good time, but not me. From now on, I would have to carry this heavy secret that kept me away from light-hearted evenings.

I took the tram downtown and got off at Barfusser Platz and headed back across the cobblestones to a side street. A few doors down to the left, I turned in under a sign that read, *Die Alte Bayerische*, The Old Bavarian, a restaurant and pub where I had been with Max and his friends. I thought I might see someone I knew there.

The tables were crowded with solid Swiss-German families, and the air was warm and thick with the smoke of their cigarettes and pipes. I hung my coat on a rack by the door and threaded my way through the tables to the back of the room and several large, round tables where students usually sat and drank beer. I looked around at all the faces, but there was no one there that I knew.

Walking back toward the front door, I heard a voice call my name from one of the booths along the wall. I looked around and saw a friend of Max named Urs. He was wearing the gray wool uniform of the Swiss Army. Two girls sat with him in the booth, one beside him, the other alone in the opposite seat.

Urs said to sit down, so I slid in beside the single girl. This could be good, I thought, but when Urs introduced me to the single girl, he said they were waiting for her boyfriend who was driving up from Lyons in France.

A waitress came, and I asked the others if I could buy them a drink. Urs ordered a beer and his date a coffee, but the girl beside me didn't want anything, not even a Seven-Up; after all these years, I remember offering her a Seven-Up. When the waitress left, I asked the girl if she never drank anything with alcohol in it. She said she did, but only scotch, and the only kind of scotch she liked was Chivas

Regal. She placed the accent on the last syllable of each word, Chi*vas* Re*gal.*

"You mean you can tell the difference?" I said. "Oh, yes," she said.

When the waitress came back with the beers and coffee, I asked if they had any Chivas Regal, a scotch whiskey.

"I don't know," she said. "You'll have to ask at the bar."

"Oh, no," the girl said, "you shouldn't."

"Oh, yes," I said getting up, "I'd like to."

Who was she to claim that she could taste the difference between scotches? And on top of that, who was she to like only the most expensive one? And then to top it all off, who was she to assume that I couldn't afford to buy her one? I went to the bar and asked the barmaid if she had any Chivas Regal.

"No," she said, "only Johnny Walker Red Label."

That was even better. I asked her to pour two half shots in two separate glasses. I paid and took the glasses back to the booth and put them in front of the girl.

"Now," I said, "which is the Chivas Regal?"

The girl picked up each glass and sniffed it and then took a small sip and rolled it around on her tongue. "It's this one," she said, pointing to the second glass.

"Am I right?"

"One moment," I said. "I want Urs to try."

"Which one did you pick?" Urs said, pulling the glasses across the table.

She pointed to the glass in his right hand. Urs tasted them and said he wouldn't be able to tell the brand names, but that the second one tasted smoother.

"They're both Johnny Walker Red Label from the same bottle," I said, grinning.

Urs laughed, but the girl looked at me with her mouth set tight and then turned and asked Urs' date to go to the bathroom with her. I stood up to let her slide out, and sat back down, alone with Urs.

"She's pissed," I said.

"That's all right," he said in German, "she's a screw." A screw? My God, I had blown it. I had offended this girl, and here Urs was saying that she was an easy lay. But why had he said it with such contempt? Maybe I didn't understand him right in German.

"*Eine schraube*?" I said. A screw?

"Yes," he said, twisting the tip of one thumb in the palm of his other hand, "a screw. Sex?"

"What do you mean by that?" I said. "She wants to have sex?"

"Yo, *nein*!" he said, his head snapping back, and then he burst out laughing. "it's just the opposite," he said. "In English, it means 'a bitch'."

"Ohhhh, I see," I said. "Yeah, well I agree. And I'm leaving before the screw gets back."

"OK," Urs said, "but let's finish the whiskey first."

We each took one of the glasses and downed what was left. Then I stood up and shook his hand and pointed to his uniform.

"What do you call it in German?" I said, "Government holidays?"

"You call it in English, 'A-pain-in-the-ass'."

26

I laughed and said goodbye and walked back through the smoky, crowded room to the door, where I got my coat from the rack and put it on and stepped out into the cool night air.

A movie must have let out up the street, or a performance at the Comedy Playhouse, because a stream of people flowed along the sidewalk from that direction, most of them walking in couples. The lights from passing cars lit up their faces and made the whole scene look like one from a movie: young, happy Europeans out for Saturday night fun in the city. And although I was in the middle of the scene, I felt all alone. Why had I pulled that cheap trick on the girl? If I hadn't, then at least I would have had a place to sit and be with somebody. Now I was out in the cold again, alone with the specter of the speeches, just what I had come down to escape.

What was I doing to myself? How could I have thought that my trick would be so cute? Had I really believed that the girl would think it was funny to be made a fool of, that she would somehow admire me for showing up her foolish snobbery? The answer is yes, I did believe that, and it shocked me that it did, that I could be so unaware of the effects my actions could have on people.

Now I think I can see what I was doing, and I realize now that I had done it before the night in Basel. It was two years before, during my junior year at Vanderbilt. I was at a brunch at my fraternity house, a special brunch given by the Nashville members for their mothers.

"You? In a fraternity?" some of you are saying. Yeah, why not? Although now it even seems weird to me, fraternities, sororities, luncheons for mothers, yech! But hold on for a second and I think you'll see the sense in it.

At the brunch that Saturday, I sat at a table with a guy named Charley and his mother and a couple of other mothers; whose they were, I don't remember. Charley had always attended private schools. He had a wide smile, a strong jaw, and even a chin with one of those dimples in the center of it that used to be called a mule's butt.

He wrestled for the fraternity in intramural competition, and he played on the fraternity football team. And Charley's mother? Well-dressed, well-preserved, well-heeled, and most certainly, well-bred.

And then I? I? Well, I had grown a beard that semester. It's hard now to think of what a beard did to people in those days. For example, at one party I went to, a local candidate for federal judge told me I was the kind of person who was ruining Vanderbilt. To make his point, he kept asking me why I was the only one at the party who wore a beard. Another student pointed out that the judge was the only one there with a polo shirt on.

"Aw, it's not the same, and you know it," the judge had drawled, and before the evening was over, he had even drunkenly shoved me.

Anyway, poor me. At the fraternity brunch, Charley's mother asked me about the beard; she wanted to know why I had grown it. At first, I said something about just wanting a change, but then I went further in my defense. I told her I had a picture of my great grandparents' fiftieth wedding anniversary, and all the men in it were wearing beards. I was hoping, I guess, to show that if all those old, conservative Southerners wore beards, then I wasn't such a screaming revolutionary for doing the same.

"Oh," she had said, "Do you look like any of them?"

Did I look like any of my male ancestors? Did she realize the nasty implications of that remark? I looked at her, but couldn't see any indication she did, but I wasn't going to let it pass. And here comes another one of those remarks welling up that I thought would get a big laugh.

"No," I said, "I looked like the milkman."

"Oh!" she said with a thin smile, and she looked away.

"That wasn't very nice," Charley said without smiling, and I could see the large muscles of his square jaw flexing.

"Well, Charley," I said, "what do you want me to do, apologize?" And apologize is just what I wanted to do, because their appalled reaction appalled me.

But I couldn't. To apologize would mean admitting that I had done something to apologize for, and I couldn't admit that. It was only a joke, for Christ's sake!

But now, with my super-analytical circling method, I think I've unearthed what it was that I was doing, if you can say "I" for the part of me that's not always available to conscious awareness. I was indirectly defining to myself who I really was by setting myself off from the people I wasn't. For the first time in my life, I was climbing down from the bandwagon of the snobs and pretenders, the social-climbers and the class-conscious right-clubbers, and finding out that I had never really belonged there in the first place.

But the trouble was, I didn't know that's what I was doing; so at the same time, I was holding on, scared. And the harder I held on, the more drastic measures the other me had to take to pull me off.

So, once again, I'd like to call out to the younger me standing there that Saturday night on that Basel street, calling more gently this time, "It's okay, Wallace. Don't worry. It's all coming from you. You'll just have to sit back and accept your own divisiveness while it works itself out."

But I wouldn't have wanted that knowledge then. Somehow it would have been too scary to know I was doing something to myself that was largely out of my control. And what do I mean, it *was* too scary? It often still is.

Now, I'd better let me turn and walk back down the street the way I came. I needed a drink something fierce, and I wasn't about to go back into the Alte Bayerische and face that scorned and scornful woman. There was another bar on Barfusser Platz where I went sometimes and drank and talked to the barmaid when things weren't busy.

I crossed the square to the bar and looked in through the large, plate glass window. Good, the place was packed. I'd shove on in and maybe get some of that Saturday night feeling I saw all around me, even if I had to get it through osmosis.

I opened the door and felt a wall of smoke and noise hit my face. The booths along both walls were full, with three or four people in each seat, and straight ahead at the bar, customers stood two or three deep.

I plowed into the crowd and edged in as close as I could to the bar. I ordered a beer over a shoulder, and then I pushed in sideways when one of the people at the bar backed out. The bartender brought my beer, and I drank it quickly and ordered another. The girl I knew wasn't working, but I didn't mind. It was enough just to be standing there surrounded by all those shouting, laughing people.

Held against the bar by the pack of bodies, I drank my beer and began to feel a pleasant, floating sensation. No one talked to me or looked at me, and I got the feeling that I was invisible. As long as I didn't do anything to shock anyone, like jumping up on the bar and howling out my fear and loneliness, I could stand undisturbed and drink myself blind, almost as if I had the bar to myself.

And that was a good feeling, not to be noticed, not to be on trial, not to be *up* for anyone or anything, not performing or fearing a future performance. The great world of fear and obligation, duty to make speeches, to be somebody, to make something of myself; the world of all those phantom judges and people I might let down began to shrink back into me until it was just a small circle about six inches across, a zero, which was me, and that was a comforting thought.

I could have passed out or died and no one would have noticed. All the other bodies would have held me in place at the bar until closing time. Sure, my parents would have mourned, the Rosslers would have, too, but everyone else would have gone on without missing a step, and this, too, was a comforting thought, a short whiff of freedom.

So, I took the small zero of myself, the only mark I had to make on the world, and the only mark it could make on me at that moment, and I placed it just above my head, letting it glow while I drank the beer, my shiny halo from a bottle.

3

If last week was a time to image dead ends, then today is death itself.

I feel absolutely worthless, truly a zero, a nothing, a waste of protoplasm and bone marrow. I hardly even have the energy to hate myself.

"Take responsibility for yourself!" my inner judges scream. "You are what you choose to be! Do you want to know what you want in life? Just look at yourself. You've got it!"

If they're right, then I wanted to be a timid bozo who's afraid of his own shadow, a failure, a miserable nobody. What's hardest to take, I've got abilities, intelligence, even good looks. And yet it's wasted on me; I'm rotten to the core. Worse yet, I'm empty at the core. An arid, empty place where no wind blows.

I've told myself for years that I want to be a writer, but I always set things up so that I didn't write. I didn't have time; I had to earn a living; I just didn't have the proper environment. Now I know that if you're going to write, you will write, and if not, you won't, and just about any environment will work, even sitting here in the library feeling contempt for all the students getting ready for finals, all of them so full of purpose, frenzied with preparation, stupid with the intensity of rote learning.

And I sit here waiting for divine inspiration to grab me by the brain and tickle me into an ecstasy of creation. When it doesn't come, I write anyway, hoping that after getting enough sludge down, enough dross, I'll break through to the refined stuff, the pure silver and gold.

But every word I write is like chewing cold ashes, and it's even worse when I don't write, so here come some more ashes. Gag, ahghh. Smack your lips, you whining bastard. Rub your nose in it. It's time you faced yourself. Of course, you hate these students. They have a purpose in life, while you're locked to this desk, and pen, and piece of paper, and it's all for nothing. You hate what you're doing, and you don't want to do anything else. Whoever told you that you could write? Too many people for your own good. One was already one too many. Why did they fill my head with these foolish, impossible dreams?

Still, I write.

I'm afraid not to. If I quit, I'd have to admit what a farce I've been living for all these years. At least this way I can bring home a stack of newly filled pages every night to that miserable shack beside the tracks, and my wife will think I'm up to something worthwhile. Christ! A pregnant wife and a dead-end life at thirty-five.

"You!" you cry out in shock. "*You* have a wife? You mean a nut like you could get someone to marry him?"

Yeah. That's right. And not just any old someone either; she's special in so many ways. As an old friend of mine told me after he met her, "Wallace, you must have something that don't show."

I told you I have certain things going for me; that's part of the problem; these certain things are going to waste.

And now a little one is on the way, which is all the more reason for me to get my act together, better still, to drop this self-divided act once and for all.

Sometimes it seems that I've been wasting all my time and energy since my return from Basel trying to figure out what happened to me. Everything in my life seems to begin with that crack-up, while other things were ending with it.

That's what I mean by *circling*. Round and round again, covering the same ground. And what good will any explanation do, anyway? Maybe nothing, maybe a lot. Maybe if I can get it fixed on paper, then I can forget it.

And then what? Who knows? Maybe I could hawk it in New York as a book. But who, I ask you, who would want to hear these wretched cries from the bottom of the heap, this bitter whining from the empty edge of the heartland?

Not that it matters. Even if no one wants to read it, and even if no blinding flash of revelation comes, I'll still have it down in writing, and if nothing else, I'll be able to cram it in a drawer and forget about it. So, let's get on with it.

Where was I? In a bar in Basel, drinking myself sane. And as I look back over that year, searching for clues to tell me what went wrong, the first screwup I fasten on is the amount of drinking I did. It strikes me now as some kind of a sign that I drank a lot my very first day in Basel. In fact, I had a drink in the early afternoon when I met Herr Rossler at his office on the Sanktalbananlage. I remember I had Campari for the first time, a Campari-soda, and I can still taste its bitter-sweet spiciness and feel the pleasant sense of strangeness that drinking it in the new surroundings gave me. I was sitting at a large, polished conference table, and Herr Rossler mixed it himself at a sideboard across the room that had a full set-up of liquor bottles and glasses on it.

Then later, at the Rosslers' home, I'm sure we had wine at dinner. Herr Rossler kept a room in the cellar stocked with wine, and they drank a bottle every night with dinner.

After dinner, Heiner, a friend of Max who attended the Basel Gymnasium with him, came over and took Max and me for a ride in his Deux Chevaux down through the hilly, winding roads in the Jura Mountains south of Basel.

We stopped at a roadside inn and bought several large bottles of beer to take with us on the ride. I can still see the bottles clearly, perhaps because I emptied so many like them that year. Clear glass liter bottles with white, ceramic tops ringed with red rubber gaskets and fastened to the bottle necks with heavy wire clamps, so you could reseal them to keep the beer from going flat. But we hardly ever gave ourselves the opportunity to utilize this clever device.

Heiner sang lead in Max's rock band, and he also wrote songs the band played, and that night was just the first of many that I drank with Heiner and Max.

Max and Heiner's band practiced down in the Rosslers' cellar in a room Herr Rossler had soundproofed by covering the walls and ceiling with open egg cartons. Usually, toward the end of a session, I'd get a beer from the fridge and take it downstairs and listen to the final play-through of the songs the band was working on. Then, we'd walk down to the restaurant at Neuweilerplatz and drink a few more beers.

On Saturdays, Max and I would often meet Heiner downtown at the Alte Bayerische for a beer, and then we'd go listen to Dixieland Jazz at a small place that didn't sell alcohol. Afterwards, we'd go back to the Alte Bayerische and sit at one of the circular tables and drink with friends of Max and Heiner from school.

But the night of drinking that put all the others to shame was one Saturday in late fall. Heiner had arranged a blind date for me, and we planned to go out after dinner to Klein Basel, the part of town across the Rhein, to a club where we could listen to music and dance.

I felt more than ready to get out of the house; a steady rain had kept me in all day reading.

The Rosslers were going out, too, for dinner and a play, and Max, as usual, was at his girlfriend's place. Before leaving, Frau Rossler prepared a small dinner of cold cuts and set it out at my place on the table. Then they were gone and I had the place to myself. Before I sat down to eat, I went to the fridge and got a small bottle of beer and took it into the living room. I put one of Max's albums on the stereo, the Jimi Hendrix album with "Hey, Joe," and I stood at the front window drinking the beer and watching the rain drip from the wet leaves. What was I thinking about? Why, the girl I'd left behind, of course. By then, she had stopped writing, and I was worried that she was the one who was doing the leaving. But hold on, I'll get to that soon enough.

When I finished the beer, I got another and took it to the table. I sat and ate, taking my time, thinking of how it would be with the blind date, wondering if anyone in Basel could be as horny as I was.

After eating, I went back to the living room, to Herr Rossler's liquor cabinet, and poured a shot glass full of scotch. I turned up the volume of the stereo and played both sides of the Hendrix album. When Heiner came, I got him a beer, and we listened to the album again.

After that point, the evening comes back to me in broken bits, separated by large gaps in my memory: Heiner stands across the Rosslers' living room, laughing while I dance to Hendrix. My date, a tall, large-boned girl with short, blond hair is bending down to get in Heiner's car. She's wearing a gray suit with a knee-length skirt, and she has on sturdy, high-heeled shoes.

Now, we're dancing in the club across the Rhein. It's dark and I hold her close. Then, I'm standing at the bar without the girl, talking to three Yugoslav men in German. We make a toast, "*Zhiva Tito!*"

36

Long live Tito, and I shout two other words I picked up on a trip through Yugoslavia, "*Raznichi!*" "*Kavovchichi*", the names of kabob dishes.

Now, Heiner is telling me he's taking the girls home. Suddenly, he's back. I leave with the Yugoslavs. Heiner and the bartender catch up with me outside and tell me I owe a lot for drinks. They say I had bought the house a round. I fumble in my pockets, come up with my house keys and try to give them in payment. Heiner says he'll take care of it.

Dimly now, very dimly, I watch the reels of a tape deck revolve, and someone talks of jazz. Then, as if in a dark tunnel, I see a man in the light of a street lamp, walking toward me down a cobblestone street. I'm talking to him in a loud voice. Next, I'm in a very small room, jumping up and slamming my fists against the ceiling. I hear a voice coming from the closed steel door of the room, and I see the eyes and nose of a man in a small, square opening in the door. I stumble to the door and beat on the steel, yelling at the man. He closes the opening. Finally, I'm lying on a small platform on the floor which is padded and covered with leather upholstery. Two men in blue uniforms stand over me.

"*Ich habe kalt,*" I say to them. I'm cold. One of them leaves and returns with a blanket, tosses it over me.

"*Danke Schoen,*" I mutter.

The next morning when I woke, I realized I was in jail. I sat up and looked around. There was nothing in the room but the raised platform I was sitting on and a urinal on the wall. I was struck with how clean and well-made the room and the two fixtures were for a drunk tank. I could barely remember jumping up and down in the cell.

A cop in the blue uniform came and opened the door to the cell and looked in. He told me to come with him, and we walked side by side down a corridor with other steel doors at even intervals along the walls. The corridor led into a large office with several desks. We went to one of the desks, where another policeman sat, with a passport lying in front of him. It was mine. He picked it up and looked at me.

"You know why you're here, don't you?" he asked in German.

"Apparently," I said, and shrugged. But it came to me later that I really didn't know. I knew that I'd been drunk, yes, but what had I done to provoke the cops? There was a lump on the top of my head; had I been fighting? Or had I passed out and fallen head-first into the gutter, so that all the police had to do was gather up my limp carcass and haul it in and dump it in the tank? Or did I dig in my heels and invite the lump from a police billy? I never learned the answer, and sometimes even now, I get a twinge of guilt and fear in my stomach when I think of that stretch of lost hours.

I can remember walking down a street in the early morning after they let me go. I needed a shave, and I felt like I would seem a bum to the proper Baslers on their way to church. I had planned to go with the Rosslers to see their daughter, Rosemarie, at her school in the French part of Switzerland, but when I got to the house, they had already left. I climbed the stairs to my bedroom, undressed and crawled in under the covers.

The next thing I remember is Max knocking on my door. I told him in a weak, sleepy voice to come in. He peeked around the edge of the door and asked how I was. I said okay, considering I had spent the night in jail.

"Jail?" he said, and grinned.

"Yes," I said, "But don't worry, it was a nice one."

Max laughed and ran down the stairs to tell his parents. He thought I was making a joke about the jail's being nice, but I hadn't been. It was my way of softening the blow of their finding out I had been jailed.

Frau Rossler brought up a pot of tea and poured me a cup. It was steeped in a combination of herbs that she called "nerve tea," and I was to have it more than once as the year passed.

When I went downstairs before dinner, Herr Rossler was sitting back in his easy chair in the living room, having an aperitif. He looked up at me and smiled, then reached out his hand to shake mine.

"Still alive?" he said in English.

"Just barely," I said, and I felt a rush of gratitude at the way all of them had taken the news. I mean, after all, I had gotten knee-walking, toilet-hugging *drunk*, and landed in *jail*, for Christ's sake, and I was supposed to be a goodwill ambassador for the United States of America and Rotary International!

Frau Rossler told me later that Herr Rossler made a discreet inquiry at the police station in Klein Basel and found out that nothing serious had happened before the cops took me in, and that there would be no permanent record of arrest. That didn't stop my worrying, though, about what had happened during the times I couldn't remember.

Once, when I was going over it again, trying to reconstruct the evening, an embarrassing thought occurred to me. Why had I left a girl, to talk to men at the bar? Well, things weren't going well with her, and I was so drunk I just wanted to raise a little hell with the boys, like I used to at Vanderbilt.

But the thought persisted. Why would I leave the club with three strange men? Well, Jesus, like I said, to raise hell, to have a good time; maybe I thought I could find another girl, one as horny as I was.

But what if...I pushed the thought away, but it shoved its way forward again. What if, oh God, what if those guys had knocked me out and then, Christ, what if they had stuffed their pricks up my ass or, *aaagh*, down my throat! And Jesus Christ, what if they hadn't even had to knock me out!!!

I had just been reading Mailer's *Advertisements for Myself,* and I remembered something he said about a period of depression he experienced. He attributed it to latent homosexuality at work in his psyche, and I thought, *Mailer,* this hard-assed guy who was always going around getting men to arm-wrestle, a latent homosexual? What a chilling concept, the *latent* part. I mean, if you are something and you know it, fine, but it scared me to think that some professional could slyly find out something about me that I didn't know about.

And then if you're afraid of something that may be there, isn't that a sure sign that it *is*? Was this what was making me feel I had something to hide? Was this what caused all the fear when I got up in front of strangers? Was I a flaming closet queen, and all these years, even I hadn't known it?

But then I remembered something else I had read, a passing reference to the possibility of Nietzsche's having homosexual tendencies. What I had read played down the claim, pointing out that after Nietzsche suffered his final breakdown, he would ask friends to bring him a woman. Also, the writer said Nietzsche's dreams were of women, and remembering that, I breathed easier, for my dreams, too, were of women.

But still, I had to wonder, where in hell did thoughts like that come from? Why was I tormenting myself with all these awful self-doubts?

* * *

4

L ast night, Ellie was late coming home. It was five o'clock, and the winter sun had already set, so that it seemed even colder than it really was in this damp little shack by the ocean. It rained yesterday, and the dirt street that runs between the house and the tracks was turning into mud, making even a walk unpleasant. So, there I was, stuck inside with cabin fever, smelling the wet-dog smell from the damp carpet and just waiting.

Where was she? She said she was going to do some Christmas shopping after school, but she's only teaching half-days, so she really should have been home before dark. I decided to take a run through town on the street.

It's not as nice as the beach, but I just wasn't up to fighting the mud on the trail down the cliff. I've skied down that way every year during the rains, but I don't risk it in the dark.

It was cold out, so I put on a sweatshirt and sweatpants and a wool watch cap. Walking down our mud street, I stayed under the row of cypress trees, where the fallen needles gave some dry footing. At the end of the block, I turned right where the paved street starts and stepped off at a slow jog.

At the first corner, I stopped to watch the headlights of a car pass in a hissing roar. Idiot! Why all the hurry on these wet streets? All he's probably speeding home to is a night of electronic catatonia in front of the TV.

As I ran, I looked at the houses on either side of the street, and I could see silhouettes of humans in their chairs in the darkened rooms, immobilized, watching the dancing, gesturing, colored forms on the screens. Another car roared past from behind me, and I watched the reflection of its tail lights recede down the street with the dying whine of the engine.

God, I hope none of these fools crashes into Ellie. What would I do at this time of my life without her? Could I even go on? That question made me feel lost and bleak.

But when I got back to the end of the pavement and turned onto our street, I looked down the row of identical shacks and saw her car in front of ours. I felt a thrill like I was going on a first date, but that didn't last long. When I walked in, she was in the narrow passage we call the kitchen.

"Hey!" I said, smiling, "I was worried about you." She turned and looked at me without smiling, her arms hanging at her sides. Then she turned back toward the sink, dropping her head and bringing one hand to her face.

"What's the matter?" I said.

She gripped the edge of the counter with both hands and said in a breaking voice, "I didn't even want to come home." Then she started crying,

"Woo-hoo-hoo-hoo," long sobs that she tried to talk through. "Everything was finally too much. This house is so cold. It's just a dump, and it's Christmas and we don't have any money. And look at your hair; it looks like a freak. Woo-hoo-hoo-hoo."

I put my arms around her and said, "Look, it'll be all right. I've been running. I wore my watch cap and my hair's stuck down with sweat."

But she didn't want to be comforted. She wanted to cry. Hormones. It's the hormones of the first trimester of pregnancy. We read how they cause terrific mood shifts. But that's a cop-out, and I know it. What she said next showed me what a cop-out it is.

"You said last night you're a failure."

That's right, I did. I've got to stop this whining to her about my wretched inner life, especially now that she's pregnant. But she wasn't finished yet.

"I know if I want all those things and a better life, I can get them for myself, but all I wanted today was for someone to give it to me. I wanted my mother to come and take care of me. Woo-hoo-hoo-hoo."

No, it wasn't just hormones; it was the life I've been living, locked up in this dump or clinging to a desk seven stories in the air at the central library of UCSD, scratching little squiggly lines on page after page of paper. As Ellie talked, two pictures grew in my mind. The first was a different image of Ellie, of that part of her life that I've never known, as a daughter of the upper middle class who has expectations of a husband who will take care of her. The other image was of me and my myth, my "destiny," the pattern of winning only to lose, that I wrote about. And my reaction to the two pictures surprised me.

Instead of resenting Ellie for demanding that I be more than I am, I began to resent what I've been, a helpless self-defeater. And I got a scare that the pattern I've described is repeating itself in my life with Ellie. First came the wooing and the winning, and now comes the losing. I picked a banker's daughter, and now I'll get her to reject me by creating a life she can't live.

Another surprise was that I wasn't just scared, I was pissed off at myself. Instead of wanting to tell her that I'd never live up to her expectations, and that she'd better learn to stand on her own two feet, it made me want to stand on mine, to make it in the world of work. I got a picture of myself on a job site, building cabinets, even working at two jobs, one at night, teaching. Work, yes, work. What a cure for whatever ails a WASP.

And as I sit here this morning, determined to get this done and get on with my life, I realize that one of the clues that I'm searching for, one of the pieces to the puzzle of that year, was the lack of meaningful work.

Up until that year, school had provided that work for me, but it didn't work that way at Basel, mainly because their university system is different from ours. By the time the students get to college, they've done fourteen years of preparatory work instead of twelve, chosen their major, and put testing in individual courses behind. All they do is register for the semester and pay their fees, receive a *Testatbuch*, a small book to list their courses in, and go to whichever lectures they choose. No tests, no papers to hand in.

"But who's to make sure they attend class?" all the Nazis scream in unison.

"No one!" I answer. "No one polices them. Once, at the beginning of each semester, and once, at the end, the professor in each course signs their book, and that's considered proof of attendance. At the end of three years, they write a thesis in their subject and take orals, like we do for an MA. It's up to the students whether or not they will make the grade. It's a nice system for student and teacher alike; no papers to write, no tests to take, and likewise, none to grade."

But for me? My sixteen years of preparation in our system with its built-in taskmasters hadn't prepared me for that. Without assignments and deadlines, I felt like the wino without the wine, the junkie without the junk.

I went to the lectures at the university, and I read a lot, but not German literature. Instead, I read Hemingway, Faulkner, Fitzgerald. Now I look back and realize I was in Europe, I was young, I should have been having the time of my life. I could have written, written, written: poems, crazy stories, porno books, anything. Instead, I spent most of my time reading the writers who *had* written when they were young and in Europe. And the amazing thing is, I somehow managed to tell myself that I was almost living the same life, if you just left out the fact that I didn't write.

When I first got there, the new life in a strange country was enough to keep me occupied. I had the third floor of the Rosslers' to myself, a small bedroom with a single bed against one wall, an armoire on the wall opposite the bed, and a small desk underneath a double window. And since the other bedroom on that floor was empty, the bathroom was mine too.

I could look out the window over the toilet and see across the city to the wooded hills across the Rhein. The woods were the south edge of the *Schwarzwald*, and I was impressed at first that I could stand there pissing and look out over the roofs and spires of a Medieval city to Germany, thinking often of the small ads I had seen as a kid in the back of men's magazines for knives with blades of genuine Black Forest steel. And there it was!

In the mornings when I went downstairs, Herr Rossler would have already left for work, Max for school, and Frau Rossler for the marketing, but even in her absence, she managed to pamper me. She would have set my place at the table and left out a tray with a pot of hot chocolate under a tea cozy, a plate of cheeses, and another of bread slices and rolls.

After breakfast, I would head down to Neuweilerplatz to catch the tram. An old man almost always stood in front of the post office at Neuweilerplatz. He wore a gray hat and an old army greatcoat with a muffler, even when it wasn't cold. His head wobbled on his thin neck with some kind of palsy. The first time I passed him, our eyes met and I said, "*Guten Morgen.*"

Without a word, the old man pulled one hand out of a coat pocket and pointed with a trembling finger down at a basket of lemons at his feet. No nonsense here, the old man's actions said, no social bullshit, just pay or pass on. I laughed and reached in my pocket for some change. What he did struck me as funny, but I felt somehow sheepish, too, because he looked so serious. This wasn't play acting, this was *life*!

Later, when I began to have problems of my own with shaking hands, the old man didn't seem funny anymore. It was ominous to see him, it was as if I were looking into my own future. This is how I would end up, a poor, lonely, trembling old man selling lemons on a street corner. You can see that I had too much time to think.

What about the lectures? Why didn't I get heavy into German literature? In the first place, lack of interest. I just never caught fire from the Germans, especially not the ones that were the subject of courses that year.

And then I had a hard time understanding the literary German of the lectures. I even attended a class on American literature, since I found that already knowing something of the subject helped me understand what the professor was saying.

What stayed with me from the lectures, though, were small, irrelevant images of the students. I can see one in a lecture on Goethe, sitting across the amphitheater classroom from me under a tall window. What has caught my eye is a clear drop hanging from the tip of his nose as he bends over a page of paper, scribbling notes. The light from the window shines through the drop; then the drop breaks free and falls to the page. The student writes without a pause while another drop grows down to replace the one that fell.

Another image that stayed with me is of a table board from the refectory of the old University building. It hung on the wall of the coffee shop in the new building and was carved all over with names and initials, one that I knew:

F. Nietzsche.

Someone had to be putting me on! I knew that Nietzsche was a professor at Basel for ten years, but as loony as he was, I didn't think he was the type to carve his name on tabletops.

What I came to enjoy most about the university were the trips to and from it. From Neuweilerplatz, the tram went straight down a wide street lined with trees and blocks of flats. Then the left side of the street opened onto a large green sports field. Past the sports field, the tram went one more block and then turned right on its half-circle route into the center of town. There was a park at the corner where the tram turned, and I would usually get off there and walk the direct route to the university.

On my way into town, the buildings changed in style from modern to medieval, and the streets from asphalt to cobblestone, so my first sight of the university surprised me. I had expected gray stone buttresses and spires, peaked windows of leaded glass, but instead I saw a smooth expanse of yellow marble, broken only by three even rows of oblong windows rising to the wide, flat overhang of the roof. At its front, the building faced the Petersplatz, a small square with trees and park benches, and a long bike rack for the students' bikes and mopeds.

If I stayed on the tram for the alternate route into the Marktplatz, there was always something to see. On the Marktplatz itself, farmers' wives from the Alsace and from farms in Baselland set up striped umbrellas and stands where they sold vegetables and flowers. There was steady movement on the square, with trams stopping and starting, groups of students walking or riding bikes to school, and the shoppers walking from stall to stall. And me, the invisible man.

The town hall, on the side of the square near the Rhein, was a red building with a clocktower at one end. Because of its color, it was called *Das Rothaus*, the red house, instead of *Das Rathaus*, the town hall. In the sixteenth century, Hans Holbein the Younger had painted murals inside! Just around the corner toward the Rhein was Wepf's bookstore, where I spent time browsing through the Penguin paperbacks for books to read in English.

Across the square, a narrow alley called the Totengasschen, the Little Alley of the Dead, led in stairs up through medieval row houses to the Peterskirche and across another street to the Petersplatz and the university.

After dark, it gave me a spooky thrill to walk up the stair-stepped gradient of the alley and pass the deserted church. And when it rained, I always liked to turn the corner of the church and see the streetlights reflected in the wet cobblestones of the street.

Then, on my way home, if I had time to kill, I would walk back down the Totengasschen to the square and on past Wepf's to the Mittlere Bruecke, the middle bridge, and watch the Rheinboats pass. I read that in 1225, when this stone-arched bridge was built on the orders of the Catholic Bishop of Basel, it was the only one on the Rhein between Basel and the North Sea! After standing there a while, I would walk upstream toward the Muenster, a Romanesque-Gothic cathedral with two spires, the very cathedral that Carl Gustav Jung made famous with his childhood dream of its destruction by the awful descent from Heaven of God's divine bowel movement.

From the Muenster, walking away from the river, I could quickly reach Barfursserplatz, the Barefoot Square. If the weather was good, I could sit out at a table in front of the Casino and drink a beer while I watched the traffic on the square, but if not, I could cross the square to the small bar on the other side.

The city had the Fine Arts Museum and the large Art Gallery, where I once saw a special show of Klee's work. I liked his stuff. I had first seen it on small, colored postcards that my roommate in college kept pinned on the wall above his desk. One of the first things I learned from that roommate was to pronounce Klee's name to rhyme with clay and not with glee. In the exhibit, there was a series of drawings that Klee had titled. A line drawing of a chicken was called, "*Wo die Eier herkommen, and Der Gute Braten.*"

"Where the eggs come from, and good roast." At the bottom of another, a furious, dark, scribbly mass of a creature, Klee had written, "*Tanze, du Ungeheuer, zu meinem sanften Lied.*" "Dance, you monster, to my soft song."

And on the last in the series, Klee left his signature: "*Alle diese Bilder, hat der Onkel Klee gemacht.*" "All these pictures, Uncle Klee has made." Are you wondering how I remembered the titles after all these years? Did I carry little three-by-five cards even then to jot down bits of scenes, dialogue, ideas for stories that I never got around to writing? No. I wrote the titles down on a scrap of paper at the exhibit and then copied them into a cloth-bound notebook with lined pages and dark, blue-ink numbers in the upper right-hand corner of each page. I bought it when I first got to Europe for keeping a writer's journal of my experiences that year, but like my other writing projects, it fell through. Ten years later, I chopped out the few pages I'd written, one of them with Klee's titles, and put them in a file folder. I gave the rest of the book to a woman I know who really does keep journals.

Let's see, where was I? At the Klee exhibit, and as well as exhibitions, there was night life in Basel, the Stadttheater, several movie houses, and the Komödie, where I saw the premier of Duerrenmatt's *Der Meteor*.

"Wait a minute," you're saying, "you said you suffered from having nothing to do, and then you launched into a travelogue of sights and things to do in Basel that makes it look like a Paris on the Rhein."

All right. There was plenty to do for someone with initiative and a zest for life. But what I missed was having a *work* to do, what I missed was *having* to do some kind of work. And as in every other case, I filled the emptiness with full, clear bottles of beer.

Here I am again, devouring the life story of a famous person, a *Newsweek* article on the singer, Billy Joel. In it, Billy says he was lucky to have his vision fixed early, and Billy, I understand what you're saying. I, too, had a vision early on, but the trouble was, it wasn't fixed. Almost anything could displace it, and Billy, it still is a fight.

And you went through some insecure times without money, but you came through with a fierce determination to stand on your own feet? Another good lesson from the rich and famous, and *Billy*, an amazing parallel! I too have learned to do just that, even when there's nothing down there to stand on.

And Billy, *you* had some kind of breakdown at the age of twenty-one? But you completed yours, checking into a psych ward only to find out from the loonies in there that you weren't crazy after all, while I kept pushing mine away, never letting it take me as far down the road as I needed to go.

And wow, Billy, this just knocks me out! You say that your break came after some girl had let you down? Well, that's what I've been saving for now!

The sad tale of my broken love

5

Her name was Virginia, Gin for short, and I met her my junior year in college. I had come back early that year, during freshman orientation week, as a member of the freshman honorary society, Phi Eta Sigma. I held three seminars on John Kenneth Galbraith's, *The Affluent Society*. It was one of three books assigned to the freshmen to read before they got to school, the idea being to let them know right off that orientation involved a lot more than Greek rush and football rallies. Gin came to my seminar thinking it was the one on Camus' *The Plague*. After that, we saw each other around campus several times and said hi, but I never made any move to ask her out.

Then, one day I was lying out in the shade of a tree in front of the library, waiting to go to lunch down at the fraternity house. It was something I wouldn't have normally done, but the roommate who taught me how to pronounce Klee used to do eccentric, supposedly cool things like that, and I often copied him.

Actually, I wasn't comfortable doing it. A sidewalk ran up from the library and past the other side of the tree, and I was feeling self-conscious about how I looked to anyone who passed. So, I had closed my eyes and was trying to ignore the sound of footsteps on the walk.

Then I heard the muffled, thudding swishes of someone walking toward me on the grass, and a woman's voice said,

"Well, it's the Philosopher." I opened my eyes and looked up and saw Gin striding up to me. I sat up and said, "What do you mean, Philosopher?"

"You said you were a Philosophy major...in the seminar."

"Oh, yeah, I am." I stood up, brushing off the back of my pants. I noticed that her eyes were green, the greenest I'd ever seen, and her hair a dark red. I also noticed that her breasts looked large and shapely in the white cotton blouse she was wearing.

"It looks inviting here in the shade," she said, looking at me and smiling in a way that made me feel that she knew something I didn't.

"It's okay but it's not as great as it looks." I was thinking of how I could casually ask her for a date. Today was date-lunch day at the fraternity house. I could ask her to come to lunch. But what if she said no?

"Have you eaten lunch yet?" I asked.

"No," she said.

"Well, today I can bring someone to lunch at the fraternity house. Would you like to go?"

"Sure. Which fraternity?"

I told her and she said, "Oh, they're good."

"Yeah, they're all right." All right? That's right, Wallace, play it cool, but this was just what you wanted it for, so that you'd seem cool to anyone who didn't know you. You belonged to the right house, so you were somebody. God preserve you from being just you.

So, we walked together down to the fraternity house, along the tree-lined street, past the houses of the other fraternities and sororities. Gin made things easy since she always had something to say, or she always asked questions about me that I had plenty of answers for. I can't remember anything specific that either of us said on that first walk, but I still remember being conscious from the corner of my eye of the swell of her breasts in the white blouse.

Things must have gone well at lunch, because I asked Gin if she'd like to meet after classes and take a walk in Belle Meade Park. She said she would. Good. I was getting excited now. I'd walk her up to the apartment I shared with the instructive roommate and pick up a blanket.

Then, I could stop and buy beer not far from the park, and if I didn't blow it, who knows what might happen? Writing this now, I'm struck by the way I thought I controlled how and when a woman would succumb to my seductions. Oh, how quickly the scales have fallen from my eyes!

After class, Gin and I walked west from the campus under trees turning red and gold with the fall. The afternoon sun was still bright, and we came to a spot where it broke through the branches of one tree and shone down through the orange and yellow leaves. Gin was talking about my jacket, a herringbone tweed with black leather patches on the elbows. She asked me if they were real or if I had bought the jacket with them already on it.

"Already on," I said.

"Well, my mother says that you can tell the difference between a senior and a freshman because the senior's elbow patches really hide holes." She laughed and I grinned, but I was embarrassed that my patches didn't hide any holes. I remember looking down at the patterns of sun and shade on the fallen leaves and not being able to think of anything to say.

The apartment was in the upstairs of an old clapboard house on St. Charles Avenue. Our landlady lived downstairs, but we had our own outside entrance, a set of wooden steps that went up to a deck in front of the door.

When we got there, the roommate was sitting in the front room at the desk, with all the doors and windows open in the warm fall air. I introduced him and Gin, and got a blanket and a book of English and Scottish ballads, and we left.

Belle Meade Park was at the edge of a wealthy suburb with the same name. The Park road wound through hills covered with grass and trees, and there was one hill that I especially liked with a view of the surrounding hills and woods. We parked at the base of that hill and climbed to the top, where I spread out the blanket and we settled on it with the six pack of beer and the ballads book.

Lying propped up on one elbow beside Gin, I drank a beer and read several of the ballads to her, one in which a young woman tells a man (perhaps a knight) that she'll "not lie niest the wall."

"She'll not lie niest the wall," I said to Gin, suggestively.

"What does that mean?" she said, taking the bait.

"Niest means 'next to,'" I said, "And 'next to the wall' was an idiom for making love. So that meant she wouldn't make love to him."

She laughed and I went on reading, thinking that things were going okay.

She was drinking beer and she had laughed at the reference to lovemaking. She wasn't any prude, like so many of the girls at school seemed to be.

As the sun went down, we climbed back down the hill and drove and to downtown Nashville, and ate a sandwich in a small restaurant.

I must have really tried to stretch the night out, because what I remember next is standing on top of Love Circle with Gin, looking out over the lights of Nashville through a space in the trees. Whatever doubts I may have had about whether she would kiss me on the first date were gone by now, because I was holding her close against me and we were kissing, and that firm swell of breast that I had watched all day was swelling against my chest. She even let me run a hand up over them on the outside, what a rush, but only on the outside. When I tried to slip one hand in, over the top button of her blouse, she pulled back from me and took my hand away, and I could see her smile in the glow from the lights. But at least she had let me feel them on the outside.

That smile she smiled that day that seemed to show she knew something I didn't, remember? Now I know what she knew. She knew all the time what was going to happen, all the time I was guessing and hoping. She knew because she has already chosen that it would happen, and now it was simply a matter of her timing the speed at which it would. I don't think she actually plotted out consciously when she'd let me kiss her or feel her up or touch her bare breasts and kiss them; or touch her legs and then her stomach on the outside of her panties; then on the inside and further down into the crinkly delight of pubic hair, and then, and then, finally, one day we would go all the way!

No, I don't think she plotted that all out, plotted that it would take a month of what I thought was effort on my part to overcome defenses, but what turned out to be careful timing on hers, but I think now that she knew it would happen and had chosen it from the first.

And then, after that month, it would go on; we would go from just plain sex in the bedroom of that apartment to all kinds of variations: standing, sitting on chairs, squatting, bending over the brass rail of the bedstead, some clothes on, some clothes off, blowing, sucking, licking, and for danger, standing in front of the waist-high window, making love naked from the waist down. And Gin liked to dance, to strip tease, bumping and grinding, bending over and shaking her fine, firm, perfect ass at me while she smiled over her shoulder that smile; and I don't know how much of that she had foreseen, but it was certainly something for me to smile about, as well.

I don't think, though, that she foresaw the end four years later in a Park Avenue apartment in Manhattan that she and another girl were keeping for an older woman who was a friend of Liberace's. That's right. There were glossies of the old lady and Liberace in silver frames around the room. And Gin and I were lying in bed in a room cluttered with shopping bags and boxes from Saks and Bloomingdale's, when she said to me, as a way of explaining why she had gone for another man the year I was in Switzerland, "I realized you wouldn't be willing to keep me in the style to which I'm accustomed." And even though that absurd cliché sounded downright silly coming from Gin (I suspect she got it from her mother.), still, an empty, wasted feeling spread through me, and I knew that I had fallen short of her image of what I should have been, just like on the first day when I had worn a jacket with no holes under the elbow patches.

I would have loved to have kept Gin in *whatever* style, but I knew I couldn't. Something stood between me and making money, and the shaking hands and fear that had started in Switzerland were symptoms of whatever it was.

Now I wonder just how early Gin had sensed it. As much foresight as I have credited her with, I don't think it was Gin who first saw the end, but her mother. It strikes me now that Gin, on the first day we were together, told me that story about elbow patches and prefaced it with, "My mother says."

So that's what your mother said, was it? Well, I know now your mother said a lot more than that, and if I had really listened, I wouldn't have had to wait until I was all alone in Switzerland to find out what the talking meant.

The year I graduated, I spent the five days between the end of finals and graduation at Gin's home in a small Tennessee town outside of Nashville. I say I spent them at her home, but actually, Gin's mother put me up at a room in a local hotel which, by the way, happened to be one of three that she and Gin's grandmother owned.

While I was there, Gin's mother gave me a graduation present, a quote from Thoreau mounted on gold matting and framed under glass in a gilded wooden frame. It was the one about marching to the beat of a different drum. When I thanked her for it and told her I liked the quote, she laughed and said, "I really don't know why I gave *that* to you...I don't believe what it says, myself."

But I know why you gave it to me, at least I do now. I was already marching to a different beat, and this was your way of telling me you knew it.

And something else you told me while I was staying at your home (and hotel) was that you hoped I wouldn't grow a beard and start wearing sandals when I got to Europe, like some hippie. You knew I had grown a beard before; in fact, when you met me the year before, I was wearing the same one I wore to the fraternity lunch for mothers, but I shaved it off that summer when I went looking for a job.

My response was to murmur some reassurance that I wouldn't do anything like that, even though I was fairly sure that I would. The next day, my parents came through town to pick up Gin and me to drive us up to Nashville for graduation, and when my father got out of the car, he was wearing sandals.

I went back to Gin's home once more that summer, on my way to Europe, and the first night at dinner, Gin's mother told the story of what she'd said to me about the sandals, and how the very next day my father had shown up wearing sandals. "I could have just *died* for the poor boy!" she said, gasping with laughter.

I had been following along, smiling at the story, thinking she was telling a joke on herself and her own absurd association of sandals and hippies, until she said, "for the poor boy!" The joke was on *me*! I was to be pitied because my father was wearing sandals. I was supposed to have been *embarrassed* by that, for Christ's sake.

What could I say? That we had always lived in warm climates, and my old man's feet sweated a lot? That he had a problem with athlete's foot fungus, so he wore sandals to keep his feet dry? No. I kept any honest response raging around in a tight short-circuit inside my flustered skull, while I grinned at her little joke.

Now I'm amazed that with all those signs and portents I didn't see what she was trying to get across, even when Gin's grandmother stepped in to help. This was the grandmother on the hotel side, the mother of Gin's mother. She was tall, white-haired and dignified, a Virginian who said "oot" and "aboot" for "out" and "about". Also, I noticed that she repeated things she wanted to emphasize, and she had a way of speaking that *Time* and *Newsweek* like to call "sniffing". And the way she would sometimes purse her lips and draw back her nose, you would think she had caught a whiff of something foul.

Once, during my last visit, she had sniffed to me, "Some people hate snobs, but I hate people who hate snobs." Then, again, "Yes, I hate people who hate snobs," sniff. Well, all right, Grandmother, hate whomever you will, but why are you telling *me* aboot it?

I should have made the connection with a couple of other remarks she made when my parents picked me up for graduation. We were all sitting in the family room of Gin's house, having a cup of coffee before we left for Nashville, and the grandmother was telling some story about friends of hers, when she paused and sniffed to my mother and father, "They're the *railroad* people, you know." Of course, they didn't know, Grandmother. You knew they didn't, and I think you must have wanted them to feel somehow less for not knowing.

Then, when we went out to get in the car, a two or three-year-old, two-door Chevy Malibu, the grandmother took a good look at it and sniffed, "Oh, what a *nice* car." Now, what was so damned nice about it to a wealthy old lady from the *hotel* people, you know?

During all this furious barrage of elder feminine attention, Gin and I had been hard put to keep up our regimen of sex, especially with my staying nights at the hotel. But we managed: quick moments of grasping at each other in the short time I would stay after her parents went to bed, bending over quickly on the couch for a quick, scary suck on some part of the other's body, almost any part would do, but quick! And one night we got a chance to slowly jack and jill each other off at the local drive-in.

Once we went for a drive in the country, looking for a safe place to park. Outside of town, we turned the rearview mirror to a vertical position, angled down so I could see the reflection of Gin's stomach and thighs, and then she hiked up her skirt and pulled down her panties, leaving them around her knees so I could glance down and see them out of the corner of my eye while I drove, and then looking back up, I could see her bare thighs and pubic hair in the rearview.

Let me stop right here and caution anyone reading this against trying that, because even though it's exciting as hell, I'd hate to be responsible for a nationwide epidemic of car crashes in which men were found in the wreckage with raging erections, and women with their panties around their knees, and the cars' rearview mirrors all strangely at the vertical.

On the hot afternoons, Gin and I would walk alone under the heavy, green leaves of summer, past the large, white houses near Gin's to a friend's where there was a swimming pool. The friend's children had all grown up and left home, and the friend was a recluse, so we usually had the pool to ourselves.

Whenever we did, we'd change together in the dark bath house, and once or twice, we even risked getting caught in there together, and we went at it standing up.

One afternoon, on our way back to Gin's house, we passed by her great-aunt's house. Before, when the great-aunt would see us, she'd tap on a window pane and wave, but today, she came to the door and called to us to come in.

The grandmother was there, too. The two women were sisters, but you wouldn't have guessed it. The aunt was a lot shorter than the grandmother, and she talked and laughed more easily.

In the aunt's sitting room, the two women stood and talked to us with their backs to a bay window where gauze curtains diffused the hot afternoon light.

"We hear you're going to write 'The Great American Novel'," the great-aunt said to me, smiling.

"I don't know about that," I said, "but I do want to write someday." It irritated me that Gin had told them about my dream of writing.

"Well," the grandmother said, "I hope you don't write about sex."

"Well," I echoed, opening my hands out to my sides. I couldn't think of anything to say to that. Not write about sex! How could I write anything about America in the 20th century, great or not, that didn't have sex in it?

The aunt filled the awkward silence by saying, "I just read a book that handled it delightfully. The author was describing two people who'd been lovers when they were young, and this is the way he put it: 'To see them together now, you'd never guess that their heads had once touched the same pillow.'"

"Oh," the grandmother sniffed, "I think even that's too much." And then again, "Yes, even that's too much."

What was going on here? Could she read my *mind*, could she *smell* it on me? Why was I getting a lecture on not writing about sex? Did she sense some animal emanation from me that even I didn't know about? Or was I just the closest substitute around for a real writer, her only contact with that world that had gone so vulgar in her own lifetime, and the only available target for her disapproval.

Or was it just me, my family's social and financial position, or lack of it? If that was the message she was trying to get across, her final remark to me was in line with it. It came the day I left for Europe, when I was loading my bags into one of their big, white Buicks for the ride to the airport. The grandmother was standing by the front door, watching me carry the bags — two new ones I'd gotten for graduation and two battered, patched old pieces of fabric luggage that my parents had taken to Iran and back three times in six years, and once to Venezuela, and then I'd claimed them for this trip.

I had put the new bags in the trunk and was walking back to get the old ones. The grandmother stood next to the bags, looking down at them. "Oh," she sniffed, "what *nice* bags."

A crazy laugh burst out of my throat. At that moment, when I was about to leave the woman I loved, about to set out untried into an unknown world and assume, all alone, new duties to God and country and The Rotary Foundation, something inside me couldn't let me fully accept the disapproval implicit in that cracked compliment, only the humor. Nice bags, Grandmother? These were *old* bags, just like *you*, for Christ's sake, and like you, Grandmother, they weren't nice.

And now, Grandmother, I slam down the trunk of your daughter's white Buick, mercifully hiding the bags from sight, and I slam it down, too, on the part of my life I shared with you and your daughter, for I'll never see either of you again. But I will see Gin one more time in the apartment of Liberace's friend; and strangely enough, I will run into your dead husband, the hotel man, whom I never had the pleasure of meeting when he was alive.

It will be several years later, after Switzerland, after the Marines and Vietnam, and I'll be standing in the tiny one-room shack (not the one I'm standing in now) I had just rented from another old lady in my life, but she was much nicer and spiritual to boot, a friend, even, of Fritz Perls. I stand in the shack that has one whole wall that's only screen, and it's cool and dark in the shade of the eucalyptus trees that tower over the shack. And as I stand, I look at a book shelf on the wall, and I read the titles of books that someone left behind, evidently someone also very spiritual.

One of the books is a biography of Edgar Cayce, a Pulitzer prize-winning book, I learn from the cover. And that is where I meet your husband, the hotel man. That's what they call him inside the book, "The hotel man," and it turns out that your husband, who must have been a pretty spiritual guy himself, kept Cayce from starving during one part of his unusual life.

And now, Grandmother, I turn from you and get into the car, and drive to the airport. My plane takes off, and I leave your decent Southern town, never to see it again, either, except once in California when I went back to school to get money from the Veterans Administration. And one night in class, the small poet who was lecturing said that your town was where Robert Lowell went to school at "Allen Tate," camping out on Tate's lawn in a tent he'd bought downtown in a hardware store.

So maybe it has all worked out for the best; it was all working out then, but I couldn't see it. It was all trying to mean something, it still is, but I just haven't gone far enough to see exactly what. And I still had more to go even then, just to struggle on through to the end with Gin. It would be another six months or more before she'd throw her lot in with the other females, and almost two years before she'd make the final remark that showed me she saw my world through their eyes. Poor me. Poor, poor me.

Still, Gin dealt the first death blows very gently. She simply stopped writing. The Rosslers' mailbox hung on the stone wall of the raised foundation of their house, down at the base of the front steps. It was a steel box with a lock in its little door. Frau Rossler had given me a key one of my first days there, and right away I began a daily ritual of unlocking the box on my way out and then again on my way back in. Even after the letters stopped coming, it was hard to break the habit.

At first, I tried to hide the cold feeling and the fear of losing her, and I was careful not to let anything show in the letters I wrote her. I joked about her not writing, and once I sent a self-addressed, stamped envelope with a small card on which I wrote, "I am alive and well and still in love with Wallace," and I left a space at the bottom for her to sign. But all the days of turning my key in the mailbox and pulling open the door without finding anything made it too hard for me to sit down and write another letter.

I'd lie in bed at night thinking about her. Yes, yes, I'd think of her naked and dancing and shaking her ass at me; I'd think about her breasts, too. And yes, I'd jack-off thinking those thoughts, and I'd wonder who she was shaking breasts and ass at now, and what's weird, that would excite me, too, even through the jealous pain.

Was that why she didn't write? Another man? If so, I wished that she'd at least write to tell me. That would be better than not knowing, since I imagined the worst, anyway. Sometimes the frustration of facing such a blank wall actually made me feel short of breath, and I'd get out of bed and turn on the desk light and read.

Finally, I had to do something; I had to *act*. One morning, I checked the mailbox one more time and then walked down to Neuweilerplatz to a small flower shop. The girl behind the counter smiled when I said I wanted to wire a dozen roses to America, but I didn't feel like smiling back. For the card that would be sent with the flowers, I had them wire, "What the hell is going on?"

Five or six days later, when I opened the box on my way in from classes, a letter was there from Gin. It was a very short letter, but it was good enough for me. As well as I can remember, which is pretty good, it read:

Dear Wallace,

When I got to my room tonight, your roses were waiting for me, and they made me realize what I've been doing. For the past few weeks, I've been on a gay merry-go-round, dating too much and neglecting my studies.

But the roses and the card have shocked me out of all that, and now I want to get off.

But it's late now, and I'm too tired to think. I'll write more tomorrow.

I love you,

Gin

So, she *was* dating. Knowing that gave me a strange, pleasurable thrill of heartache. Had she been having sex, too, sprawled out on her back while some stranger slammed it to her, and she breathed out, "Fuck me, fuck me," like she used to do with me? Is that why she was too tired to think? She'd been out late, screwing her brains to oblivion, and she didn't have anything left for me? So, what if she had been? Just so things weren't over between us.

I was ready to find a longer letter the next day, but there was nothing in the box. The next day there was nothing for me either, and then the next day, nothing, and finally, nothing.

This time it didn't take me as long to quit writing. November passed, and half of December, and then one afternoon I was alone at the Rosslers', and the phone rang. When I answered, the voice of an American operator said she had a person-to-person call for me. Who was on the other end? Gin. Gin.

What to say? How to act? Play it cool? Be careful.

I don't remember the actual words of the conversation, but she did say that she'd be willing to crawl to me if I'd just take her back. I do remember my reply to that, because it still makes me cringe with embarrassment to think of it. I sniffed haughtily, like her grandmother, "Well, that will be awfully hard, since we've got the Atlantic Ocean between us." But she ignored my silly remark, and kept right on talking.

She was calling from her sorority house, standing in the closet, she said, to get some privacy from the other girls. I settled into a warm, triumphant feeling that she was mine again. She talked for an hour, long distance from the States to Switzerland–think of it! Think of the starving kids in India who could have been fed with the money she pissed away through the Transatlantic Cable, her parents' money, thank God, not mine.

And it came out that her new boyfriend was getting called up in the draft. He was practically failing out of school. How could she be so honest? As much as she talked of crawling, she knew it didn't matter what she said, that's how. A little embarrassment, that's probably all she felt, more from dating some prick with bad grades than at having to ask forgiveness. She knew she could have me any time she wanted. Oh, poor simple me. She hung up after promising to write that night.

A few days later, I was sitting in my room reading when Frau Rossler came up the stairs and knocked on my door. When she came in, she carried an open letter in her hand.

"Wally," she said, "I don't know what to do." She sat down on the edge of my bed.

What now? Eyeing the letter, I put my book down in my lap. "What is it?" I said.

"I thought and thought and now I have to tell you. This letter is from Gin's mother." (*Oh my God, now what?*) "She asked me not to tell you, but she wants to buy you a cake for your birthday. Look, there's this." She held up a twenty-dollar bill. "I had planned to bake you a cake myself. I'll leave it up to you."

I told her I'd rather have a homemade cake than a bought one.

"Good," she said. "Then you take the money and buy something for yourself."

This was almost too good. Gin on the phone for an hour, and the older generation in a sweat to see who would let me eat cake. But what had upset Frau Rossler so? I guess it was the fact that she had been brought into what she already knew was a sticky affair.

Gin's mother also sent me a birthday card. This was the week before Christmas. After that, nothing came from either of them, and no explanation why. I would make one last try with Gin two years later in New York on a weekend liberty from the Marines. And then, after that, nothing ever again.

* * *

6

This morning, when I was running on the beach, I saw a girl in the distance, headed my way. I glanced routinely at her as I got closer, checking her out to see if she was going to add something special to the day, and then I did a heart-catching double-take. Was she *naked* from the waist up? No, she had a towel around her neck, and she clenched the ends of it with her hands as if she were covering her breasts, but she wore a flesh-colored tank suit and a pair of cotton, draw-string pants.

Just before I reached her, she dropped her hands from the towel and swung them as she walked. The towel ends jiggled with each step she took, and when her eyes met mine, she smiled. I smiled back, and then my heart jumped up in my throat again as my eyes slid over her wet curly hair and bare shoulders and the bare side of a naked breast that jiggled beneath the towel in time to her steps. There wasn't any tank suit! She didn't have anything on above the pants but the towel!

Ah, you sweet enigma. Thank you and curse you, whoever you are. Thank you for revving up my engines, for sending a wave of sexual energy through my guts down to set my knees quivering. Curse you for the fuse you blow at the same time. How do I read the message? Are you a free California spirit who just took a swim naked, and you dig the cool air on your skin? You don't really mean to be provocative; you just want to be allowed the freedom to do and dress as you please. After all, I can run without a shirt and nobody thinks that I'm signaling to get laid. Or, are you strutting along with your breasts out because you *do* want to get laid? Or do you just want me to eat my heart out?

"*Wallace,*" a small voice in my head says, "*why not ask?*"

Well, she has the right to dress however she wants without...

"*Bullshit. Chickenshit. You're just afraid.*"

All right. You're right. I'm afraid. It's my Fear of Feminists. I don't just go around asking strange women on the beach why they're topless. I'm a little too conscious for that. In fact, my classes at college in the last few years have raised my consciousness so high that my hair often stands on end.

I've been warned. In a seminar in British fiction, a woman graduate student pounded her palm on the table and told us, "Women aren't just dogs, you know. They aren't just *cunts*!" We knew, we knew, and since a bitch is a female dog, it follows that women aren't bitches, either, or kittens or pussies, or chicks or foxes or pigs or even tomatoes.

So much trouble over the fact of being sexually attracted to women—that too was one of my big problems in Basel. I could sense something in the air, a feeling that Queen Victoria was alive and well and hissing at me every time I tried to *get some*.

There were girls, women, but no sex. The young women dressed like their middle-aged mothers, in straight skirts of dark, heavy fabrics, plain dark sweaters, and they wore nylons and low-heeled shoes like my short, dumpy grandmother wore. Not that there weren't any women who wore stylish clothes or bright colors. But they were the exceptions, and even they carried themselves in plate-glass bubbles of reserve.

Even when I was with a consenting adult woman, though, society conspired against us. Once, I went to Bern to see a Swiss woman I'd met skiing, a young ski teacher. It was a frustrating affair; she had made me promise that when we were making out, I wouldn't try to make love to her, because she was always so lost in the passion of it all, she knew she wouldn't be able to refuse. And I kept my promise!

She was staying with friends in Bern, and I got a room in a small hotel in the old town, and we'd go up to my hotel room at odd times to passionately refrain from having sex. The feeling I'd get then just came back to me, a romantic ache of desire and impending loss.

She wore a dress during that visit that I really liked, a silver, long-sleeved, shirt-waisted dress that buttoned up the front. I'd unbutton it to her waist, and we'd sit on the edge of the bed and kiss, and I can still see the way her long hair fell down over the open front of her dress and her bare breasts, oh!

One night, after we'd been in my room, we were walking down the hotel stairs when we met the desk clerk, a thin, old Swiss-German with gray hair, and he asked if we'd been in my room. Instead of telling him it was none of his goddamned business, I said yes.

"*Das geht nicht*," he said, and he actually shook his finger at us and said, "*Nein, das geht nicht*." That doesn't go.

The words sprang to the back of my teeth, "*Es ist schon gegangen*." It has already gone, but I didn't have the nerve to say them, and besides, they weren't true. Instead, we just turned and walked on down the stairs and out the front door. The next morning, I checked out and went to a hotel where I found out that it *could* go. No, I didn't just ask if they allowed sex in the rooms. I very discreetly put it in German that I'd like to have *eine Freundin*, a female friend of mine up to my room, and the clerk said that was fine.

My major problem, though, was just not meeting the right women at the right time. Like the Scandinavian woman I met when I was skiing in the spring. We didn't get to know each other until the last night I was there, and then we only sat at a table together with mutual friends, so I soon forgot about her. But one day back in Basel, when I got home from the university, Max said that some girl had called and asked for me in Swiss-German, and she spoke with a foreign accent. It turned out to be the woman I'd met skiing, and when she called back, she said she was in Basel for the evening to visit a girlfriend, and would I like to come downtown for a drink.

I would and I did, and afterwards she drove me back up to the Rosslers' in her little sports car. We sat out in their drive, and it wasn't long before I somehow managed to get my face between her legs in that cramped little car, but when I tried to pull her over the gear shift to sit on my lap, she wouldn't do it.

I remember she had on black lace panties, and they were down around her knees while she held back on her side of the car. The inside of the car windows was steamed up from our breathing, and once she said, "You must have been eating pepper tonight," and I thought, "Shit, have I got bad breath?" and I said, "Why?"

"Because you're so hot," she said, and I still feel foolish for not catching the joke. But I never saw her again, and I blamed it on not being able to take her into the house and make decent love instead of this car seat, driveway groping. Why didn't I? Why didn't I take her downstairs and be joyful among the wine bottles or on the cafe chairs in Max's band practice room?

Frau Rossler. I was afraid of Frau Rossler.

Once, earlier that year, a girl I knew from Baton Rouge was coming through Basel, and Frau Rossler had said she could stay in the empty bedroom next to mine. "But Wally," she had said, very seriously, "You must promise me you won't bring sex into my house." I did promise, and once again, just as I had with the girl in Bern, I kept my promise.

So, there I was, a young American in Europe. I had read Hemingway, Fitzgerald, even a scrap of Henry Miller when I was a kid, in an expurgated paperback edition my father had. All the sex scenes had been replaced with long lines of periods, so that just when you were getting worked up over something like, "and then I stood her on her head and . . . ." there would come all those periods.

But I knew what all the dots meant, and Hemingway's heroes had known, too. They had screwed around all over Europe, in hotel rooms in Paris, beside Italian lakes, in the mountains of Spain, and here I was wasting a whole year not bringing sex into a nice home in Basel.

It wouldn't have been so bad, probably, if Frau Rossler hadn't already been having trouble with Max. She didn't like his girlfriend because she thought the girl wanted to catch Max for his father's money. It freaked her whenever Max would come home really late and there was a chance they could have had sex. It would be just like this girl to get pregnant so that Max would have to marry her.

Once, standing downstairs in the dining room after breakfast, she told me that she had found a pair of Max's underwear with blood on them when she was doing the wash. "I showed him," she said, "but he denied me. He *would* lie to me. He said he'd hurt himself on his *bicycle*. But how? How could he hurt himself that badly and not need to see the doctor?"

I tried to stay out of their fights, but I was drawn in myself when I started dating the girlfriend's younger sister. Max had taken me down to meet her on a Saturday afternoon that fall, to a row of flats down the hill from the Rosslers'. The girls lived with their mother in a downstairs flat with a small garden in the back. Max introduced me to the two sisters and their mother in the front room of the flat, and then we all went out back and sat at a table in the garden. It had been a sunny day, and now the late afternoon sunlight filtered down through a line of trees at the back of the garden. The younger sister, Freni, went inside and came back out carrying a tray with beer bottles and set it on the table. She poured us each a glass, and after Max raised his glass to us and said "*Proshti*," we all raised ours and drank.

At first, it had been hard for me answering the women's questions in German, but after I drank a couple of glasses of beer, I began to loosen up and speak with less effort. I thought of a professor of German I met my last year at school. I had asked him if I could sit in on a graduate seminar he gave in German, so I could get used to hearing different accents before I went to Switzerland.

"Do you drink beer?" he had asked me.

"Yes," I said.

"Then don't worry about it. If you drink beer, you'll get along just fine."

And he was right. Here I was getting along just fine. I even made a wise-crack in German that everyone laughed at. Not because it was funny, but I think it just amused them to hear me trying out one of their slang sayings.

It went, "*Wein auf Bier, das rate ich dir. Bier auf Wein, das lässt sich sein*," which means the same thing as "Whiskey on beer, never fear; beer on whiskey, pretty risky."

When Freni laughed, I noticed that her teeth were crooked, but that didn't bother me, because otherwise, she was pretty good-looking. That explained, though, why she smiled with her lips together most of the time; she must have been self-conscious about her teeth. What was important to me was that she *was* smiling at me, quite a lot, and that she looked at me with a thoughtful gaze. That, and the way her ass fit so tightly in her corduroy jeans, got me hoping that the afternoon would stretch on into the night.

Just about sunset, the mother got up and left us outside. The air was cooler now, and carried the smells of dinners cooking in the other flats. The ringing of the tram bell came up through the trees at the back of the garden, and I heard a snatch of Swiss-German spoken in a woman's voice. All of it felt strange, the smells and sounds, even the trees and the last of the sunlight, but strange in a special, pleasing way.

Feeling romantic, I reached over and took Freni's hand. She put her other hand on top of mine and pressed down. I looked up at her and saw that she was smiling her closed-lipped smile. Her sister said something in Swiss-German that I didn't understand, and Freni laughed. I looked at Marie, the sister, to see if she was going to say it again in High German for my benefit, but she just smiled at me without saying anything. I smiled back, the idiotic grin that you grin when people are laughing at a joke you don't understand.

Max said it was getting cold and he was hungry, so we got up and took the empty bottles and glasses into the kitchen. Marie and Freni made sandwiches, and Max went to call Frau Rossler to tell her we wouldn't be home for dinner.

"She'll be angry," Freni said, when Max left the room.

"Really?" I said, not knowing what else to say.

"Yes. She doesn't like Marie."

"Oh," I answered, "that's too bad," when what I thought was, "Tell me something I don't already know." There was an embarrassed silence until Max walked back into the room.

Marie took a bottle of white wine out of the fridge, and Max opened it; then we took the wine and the plate of sandwiches down a flight of stairs into a dimly lit basement. There was a table in one

73

corner with a stereo on it, and two single beds were pushed against the walls on either side. Marie put a Beatles album on the stereo, and we talked over the music while we ate the sandwiches and drank the wine.

Freni and I sat with the sides of our legs touching, and I kept wondering how far this would lead tonight. It was going to be hard for me to lean over and kiss her with Max and Marie sitting there, but I knew that if I didn't at least try, I'd kick myself in the ass all the way back up the hill to the Rosslers. Max and Marie hadn't finished eating but a couple of minutes when they leaned back against the wall and started kissing. Freni and I had stopped talking, and soon we could hear Max and Marie's breathing in the pauses in the music. That should have been a signal for me to go ahead and kiss Freni, but I just sat tensely holding her hand and looking anywhere but at her. What if I tried to kiss her, and that isn't what she wanted, after all?

Finally, I let go of her hand and put my arm around her shoulder. She snuggled into my chest and raised her face. I looked down at her and she smiled her closed smile. I kissed her closed lips and they parted. Turning toward each other, we leaned back against the wall.

Just then, the sound of her mother's voice shocked us apart; she was calling from the head of the stairs. All four of us sat forward on the couches, and the girls called out in unison, "*Was, Momi*?" The mother stayed at the door at the head of the stairs, out of sight from where we sat, and told the girls that she was going out to a movie. They called goodbye, and when the door closed, they looked at each other and laughed. I breathed easier and smiled an embarrassed smile at Freni.

In a few minutes, Marie and Max got up and climbed the stairs and didn't come back. Freni and I settled back on the couch and kissed again. I ran a hand over hips on the outside of her jeans, but when I would try to slip a hand under her sweater, she'd grab my arm and stop me.

Gradually, though, she let my hand go further until finally, I unhooked her bra and pulled her sweater up over her breasts. While I caressed her breasts and stomach, she still held on hard to my arm. Leaving her sweater and bra up, I undid her jeans and pulled them down bit by bit over her hips.

All the while, we kept on kissing, and she kept her strong grip on my arm. I worked one hand in between her legs, and she began to move her hips in time to the movement of my hand. Then I took her hand and placed it on the outside of my trousers on the bulge of my penis. When she began to rub it, I unzipped my fly and put her hand on the bare skin. She opened her eyes and looked at me and breathed, "Oh, Wally."

But that was as far as she would go. We lay there for an hour, stroking each other in a trance until I had swelled up like one of the sausages I'd see hanging in the windows of the butcher shops. But if Freni felt that I was making a move to put that sausage anywhere but in her hand, she'd come out of the trance and pull away from me.

We kept on kissing and mauling each other until we heard footsteps in the room above. Then we sat up and pulled our clothes straight, and Freni got up and turned the album over on the turntable. Max came down the stairs and said he was going home, but I could stay if I wanted. I said I might as well go on up with him.

The next day, Frau Rossler seemed to be acting cooler toward me than usual. I didn't mention going to Freni's, but every time after that when she knew I was going, she'd shake her head and say something like, "Ah, Wally, you be careful."

I wanted to tell her it was okay, we weren't doing a damned thing to be careful about, which from another perspective wasn't okay at all. But I knew that wouldn't help, so I'd go on down feeling *guilty* that I was doing something Frau Rossler didn't want me to do. How could I win? She didn't want me to bring sex into her house. But she didn't want me to have sex with Freni at *anyone's* house. What *did* she want me to do? Be a *good* boy, I guess, save myself for marriage. And the real clincher was that I cared about what she wanted.

Why didn't I just move out, get an apartment downtown and do as I pleased? I don't know. Well, I do know, but I'm ashamed to admit it. Having the security of a home with the Rosslers and a substitute mother was more important than being free and on my own and having to take care of myself. So, I stayed and felt trapped and guilty.

And it didn't help when things didn't change at Freni's. In bout after bout on that basement bed, Freni always stopped me short of the final goal, even when *she* came to be the one who was going for *my* zipper. We didn't seem to have much in common other than sex, so with the frustration of not going all the way, and the guilt of Frau Rossler's disapproval, I gradually stopped seeing Freni.

What a coward, huh? What a mama's boy? Is that what you're thinking?

And on top of that, a sexist bastard who treats women as nothing more than sexual objects. Well...well...all right. You're right. Heap on the abuse. But if it makes things any better, believe me when I tell you that dropping Freni added to my burden of guilt.

What does it matter, though? The main point I'm trying to make here is that when it came to women and sex in Basel, whichever way I turned, whatever seemed to happen, I was damned to loneliness or guilt.

* * *

7

Now let's see, let's see, where am I? I've talked about drinking and latent homosexuality and the lack of a meaningful work and about heartbreak and my problems with women and sex and Frau Rossler. And now, today, I find I want to talk about not belonging. One, two, three, just like that, I'll line it all out for you, the steps to cracking up, or awakening, or whatever you want to call it.

I'm in the right mood to write about not belonging. I'm sitting in the library and it's finals time again; and once again, the place is packed with students in a silent panic of eleventh-hour preparation. They've buried themselves in stacks of books and notes that they hack away at, hoping to reduce everything to term papers by the last minute.

But they belong here and I don't. In the first place, I'm not a student here, I just use the place for free office space and books. Also, these students have a purpose, and I don't; they're going to *do* something with their education, go out into the world and get a job that they've prepared for.

But me? What am I doing here, writing these words that no one will ever read? It just doesn't make sense. I don't belong here, but I don't know of any other place where I do. I was thinking about this on my way through the woods this morning. I park on the highway on the edge of the campus so that I won't have to pay at a parking meter, and I walk in through the half-mile of eucalyptus trees that haven't been cleared yet to make way for new buildings.

And this morning, staring down at the leaves and sand passing step by step beneath me, I tried to remember when it all started. When did I first get this feeling that I don't belong? Not just that I *don't* belong, but that I *shouldn't* belong, either.

Well, it was when I was just about the same age as the people in this room, and I was doing the same things. I've already touched on it, haven't I?

It was the semester at Vanderbilt that I grew the beard. Once again, here comes that beard, threatening to take over this story, like the nose the short story by the Russian writer Gogol, escaping from my face into the streets of Nashville and rending into shreds the decent fabric of Southern society.

I've hinted that I grew the beard and made the bad taste remark to Charley's mother to prove to myself I didn't belong in their private social club. Why was I in it then? Because it was *the* thing to do, but I had to teach myself the hard way that it wasn't for me. Now, I've said I'd like to apologize to Charley and his mother for ever being there in the first place.

But who can apologize for destiny? It was my *destiny* to go all out to get into your fraternity, Charley, and my destiny as well to prove that I didn't belong, and your destiny to have just a bit of your smooth life ruffled. After all, I served a purpose in your life too; I gave it a depth it would have lacked, a failure beside which your successes could shine more brightly.

Now that's just the kind of remark that sets me off from Charley, *that* was the bad taste in the remark about the milkman. Not the sexual innuendo, but the act of putting myself down. I had made a joke at my own expense and at the expense of my own family, and in those circles, that was a shocking thing to do. The right thing was to put yourself *up*. You were supposed to be striving to be better and do better than everyone else, to be *better* and do *better*, not worse!

The reason that I'm thinking of the beard again is that yesterday a letter came from Vanderbilt. It was their first-ever survey of alumni, a questionnaire to see who is doing better and being better. The covering letter was signed by the chancellor, Alexander Heard. Now, if it had been signed by anyone but you, Alexander, I might have filled out the form, but one of the lasting grudges I bear from the semester I wore the beard is for you.

Well, I have to admit that I wouldn't fill out that form even if the covering letter had been signed by Robert Penn Warren. Where could I dredge up the nerve to check the appropriate box under INCOME BRACKET, $10,000 or less, when it's the absolute lowest category of five? And what could I put under OCCUPATION? Confessional writer? Bearer of fruitless grudges? No, I wouldn't have filled out that horrifying yardstick of what I haven't accomplished, even if Allen Tate or Dinah Shore had called me on the phone (Yes! DINAH went to Vandy!).

Nonetheless, I *do* bear a grudge for you, Alexander, and it has to do with that crazy, helpful beard. Do you remember, Dear Alex, in the spring of '65, you sat on a three-man board of interview for the Rotary Foundation to decide what Vanderbilt student would be nominated for an at-large fellowship for a year's study in a foreign country? The presidents of Scarrit and Peabody Colleges were the other two members of the board. I don't blame you that you've forgotten; I can only remember one of the questions myself: that amazing impertinence, "Why did you grow a beard?"

I didn't get the nomination, and of course I blamed the beard. The student *you* nominated, Alexander, didn't have as high a grade point average as I did, he hadn't made a university athletic team (as I had, the freshman swim team), and he didn't have a beard. In fact, the first things you *probably* noticed about him were his clean-shaven, rosy cheeks. And to top it all off, he didn't even press the nomination any further. Later, he told me that since there were only six of the at-large fellowships awarded in the world, he knew he didn't stand a chance, so he dropped out of the running. But not before he had knocked me out.

Ah, Alex, you say I'm making too much of the beard, and perhaps you're right. I've blown it up to the proportions of Margaret Mead's new dress, the "unusual and unfashionable dress that was designed to look like a wheat field with poppies blooming in it" that she wore to her first sorority rush party at DePauw. It was this dress, she thought, that got her frozen out of the sorority system and social life on campus. It remained a symbol to her of the superficiality of fraternities and sororities, and a symbol for the way organized society reacts to someone who is different. The dress is even mentioned in a short booklet on Margaret Mead's life in a series of elementary school texts that describe careers.

No one from DePauw has come forward to confirm or deny that the dress was the cause of Mead's rejection. Who would admit to being that superficial? And no one ever confirmed that my beard was the cause of my not getting the fellowship, either.

But what you don't know, Alex, is that I *did* get a Rotary Fellowship in spite of you! I applied for one of the fellowships that are awarded in the geographical districts of Rotary, and this time, without the beard.

Everything was done by mail between Nashville and Baton Rouge, so all the panel had to go on was my record and a photo of my clean-shaven face.

But that's still not conclusive proof of anything, is it? I mean, I wasn't competing against the same people. But who needs to prove anything, anyway? The point I'm making is, I was beginning to do things to show myself where I didn't belong. To quote Woody Allen quoting Groucho Marx: "I wouldn't want to belong to any club that would have me as a member." But in my case, I seemed to always want to get into the club first and then prove I didn't belong. And what strikes me now is the unconscious way I went about getting out. Just as it didn't occur to Margaret Mead to wear what the others were wearing if she wanted to be a member of their sorority, it never occurred to me that it was *I* who set up my rejection, and not the members of the clubs.

But then, most of the steps I've taken along the way toward my destiny have been unconscious. Small steps and slips of a blindfolded tree climber, groping out onto a limb. And after each fall, the bruised, blind climber gropes his way back along the roots of the tree and wraps his arms around its trunk, for in the rough caress of the bark against his cheek is the promise of another hard climb and yet another giddy fall.

How's that for poetic? Fine, but as a metaphor for your life, it's awfully scary. And even before the great fall came in Switzerland, I was learning to look and see where I didn't belong.

Not long after I got to Basel, a young Swiss woman I met at the home of a Basel Rotarian invited me to a party. She was a student at the university, and she had told me on the phone that several younger members of the literature faculty would be there, and I might enjoy meeting them.

Yes, I would, especially if any of them were young women. Yes, young worldly female professors of literature, prepared by their studies of the German Romantics to throw caution to the winds, or better still, all primed by Hemingway's novels to have a tragic love affair with a young American.

I got there a little after dark, casually dressed in sports coat and slacks. When the young woman opened the door, she had on a very dressy black evening gown, and when I walked in and looked around, I saw that all the women wore gowns and the men were wearing dinner jackets. Why hadn't she told me? I had one of the silly outfits hanging in my closet at the Rosslers. But looking back, it was better that I felt out of place from the start.

Now it's a wonder that I remember that the young woman's name was Freni, the same as Freni, the younger sister of Max's girlfriend, but it would be a safe enough bet to call her that even if I hadn't remembered what her name was. It's the nickname for Verena,

(pronounced Feraina), a popular name for Swiss girls. Usually, when I haven't been able to remember a girl's name in this book, I've called her Freni, like in the case of Max's girlfriend's sister. His girl wasn't called Marie, either, but I couldn't call them both Freni, could I?

But this young lady really was named Verena, and she was called Freni. I remember Freni's mother, a tall, wealthy lady who reminded me of Gin's mother and grandmother, telling me a story about Freni in which she was calling her Freni.

The story was about Freni's Swiss aunt who lived in England, and Freni's mother pronounced the word "aunt" as "ahnt," which to my ear always had an affected sound since I'd always heard it pronounced "ant." *Ahnt* was what snooty people like Gin's grandmother said. So, the story was about Freni's eccentric, rich ahnt in England who kept a *terrible* house, but Freni *loved* to go there because of the horses. Her ahnt had a stable *full* of horses, and Freni loved to ride. I moved on from Freni's mother as soon as I could.

Next, I listened to a group of young professors in dinner jackets, while one of them recited verbatim a parody he'd just read of Hemingway's style.

Oh, the knowing laughs he got; everyone was so bored with old H-way's stuff. It's so predictable, you know. Don't get me wrong;

there's nothing wrong with parodies. But what bothered me about this cocktail party, literary bullshit, were all these supercilious, knowing smiles. To me, they seemed to say that these cats thought they knew Hemingway or Faulkner or Mann forward and backward, and if they only wanted to, they could sit down and knock out lines of sweet-flowing prose that would show all these false idols up for what they were.

Are you getting the picture? Nothing there that I wanted to belong to, even if I did smile along with the professors. Smiling along has been my defense for most of my life. But just about then, I stopped going places where I needed to smile. Now I'd like to start frowning more.

But I'm not letting myself out of that party yet. I have to confess something I did there that shows me up to be just as false as any other fake in the room. Freni was standing next to me, and I remember thinking, "Where in hell is her *studentness*? How in hell do these Basel students jump from adolescent to frump without any transition? How do they get to be so serious so fast?"

Standing there so serious, Freni asked me what my father did. Did my heart catch with shame, was I tongue-tied for a moment while I tried to decide how to put it so it didn't sound like I came up from the working class? I don't know. What I remember telling her was that my father owned a moss plantation in South Louisiana.

"There's no such thing," you might want to say, and I'll agree with you. But that's what I told her. I said he owned a lot of land with rows and rows of old, spreading live oaks, and from the oak hangs the gray Spanish moss. I said the moss was used for furniture stuffing (it is), and that even in the watery swamps, it's harvested by the Cajuns from their pirogues. But how had I, coming from this background, gotten into the study of German literature? Well, I had an answer for that one, too.

You see, my father was very well read in French literature, because he grew up speaking French and reading the greats of France. But he had never read the Germans, and get this, he didn't trust the quality of the translations. So, he wanted me to study German and do new translations. How's that for my own brand of snobbery?

The crazy part is, while I was telling the story, I could see the old man I was imagining, sitting on the veranda of our big mansion under the oaks. A shaggy mane of white hair, and a white, General Lee beard frame his dark, Cajun good looks. He gets up and walks inside through the open French doors of the library, straight to his large, walnut desk where a leather-bound copy of *Les Miserables* lies open. He sits and pulls open a drawer, taking out note cards and a pen, and he begins to jot down new ideas for his book on Hugo.

Is that the father I really wanted? A rich, Southern landowner who was a dedicated scholar of French literature? Maybe so, at that time of my life.

God knows it was true to form that my own father's life wasn't good enough for me–almost nothing that was me or mine was.

I don't know if Freni bought the story, but she had me tell it to her mother, who was enthralled by a way of life so different from theirs, simply *enthralled*.

I thought I was pretty cute for thinking up the story, and the Rosslers got a good laugh out of it, too, when I told it to them the next day. But I couldn't have admitted then that I was ashamed to say my father was just a refinery worker. As I've already said, he was more than *just* a refinery worker, most refinery workers are. But I knew he wasn't what these people were used to, and I somehow couldn't reconcile that yet.

"Worm!" you snarl at me, "Sniveling coward!" And once again I answer, "Yes, yes, heap on the abuse." I deserve it for always running away from what I am. If you think I was trying to camouflage my background from these highbrows, you'd be amazed to see me on a building site, speaking hick to the bulls, making sure that my artistic, literary sensibilities don't show.

Well, where in hell *do* I belong? "In a nuthouse?" Is that what I heard you say? Well...yes. Maybe. That seems to be the point I'm trying to make, doesn't it? But what occurs to me now is that there's a common element in all the contrasting situations where I feel I don't belong: the feeling that I've got something to hide.

I've been looking for the external causes of my suffering, when everything may begin inside me. Sure, whatever it is was aggravated by Gin's rejection, and by all the other conflicts weaving themselves into the warp of my life. But *IT* was perhaps something in me that was trying to rise up into the light, and whatever it was, I was afraid to let it.

No, I wasn't just trying to keep wealthy Rotarians from learning what my father did for a living. Yes, in those circles I was embarrassed that he wasn't the director of a corporation, or a brilliant scientist. But keeping his job a secret wasn't enough to make me puke with fear, was it? What could all this panic mean but that whatever was coming up from the depths was dangerous, even evil?

Listen to this, from Jung's *Symbols of Transformation*:

> Experience has taught us that whenever anyone tells us his fantasies or his dreams, he is concerned not only with an urgent and intimate problem but with the one that is most painful for him at the moment.

In the footnote to this remark, Jung says:

> There is an example of this in C. A. Bernoulli, *Franz Overbeck and Friedrich Nietzsche*, I, p. 72. Bernoulli describes Nietzsche's behavior at a party in Basel: "Once at a dinner he said to a young lady seated next to him, 'I dreamed a short

while ago that my hand, lying before me on the table, suddenly had a skin like glass, shiny and transparent; in it I saw distinctly the bones, the tissues, the play of the muscles. All at once I saw a fat toad sitting on my hand and I felt at the same time an irresistible compulsion to swallow the creature. I overcame my terrible loathing and gulped it down.' The young lady laughed. 'Is that a thing to laugh at?' Nietzsche asked, dreadfully serious his deep eyes fixed on his companion, half questioning, half sorrowful. She knew then intuitively, even though she did not quite understand it, that an oracle had spoken to her in a parable, and that Nietzsche had allowed her to glimpse, as through a narrow crack, into the dark abyss of his inner self." Bernoulli makes (p. 166) the following observation: "One can perhaps see that behind the faultless exactitude of his dress there lay not so much a harmless pleasure in his appearance, as a fear of defilement born of some secret, tormenting disgust."

Nietzsche came to Basel very young; he was just at the age when other young people are contemplating marriage. Sitting beside a young woman, he tells her that something terrible and disgusting has happened to his transparent hand, something he must take completely into his body. We know what disease caused the premature ending of Nietzsche's life. It was precisely this that he had to tell his young lady, and her laughter was indeed out of tune.

Hey! Hey! That puts a different complexion on things, doesn't it? And hadn't I told a story to a young lady? Now you know you're dealing with a loony of a different color. "Maybe he *is* dangerous," you whisper to yourself. But there's a difference. Nietzsche's story revealed something fearful about himself, while mine concealed the real me. What was I hiding? What was this horror I kept down out of the light that threatened to break out when I had to speak at Rotary luncheons?

Was it the same part of me that made me blurt out offensive jokes at the wrong moment, that prompted me to grow a beard, essentially to let *pubic* hair grow on my face in public view? Whatever it was, it wasn't simply that my father worked in a refinery. What, then?

Let's look at Jung's ominous sentence: "We know what disease caused the premature ending of Nietzsche's life." What disease, Carl? Don't be coy, spit it out. *Syphilis*. At least, that's what Herr Doktor Möbius, the famous German doctor, concluded from his examination of the hospital records of Nietzsche's stays after his mental collapse. Was that my problem, too? Latent syphilis? I had gotten the clap once in Baton Rouge, but even though that was something I liked to keep quiet about, it was hardly the kind of story I wanted to keep hidden in "the dark abyss of my inner self." No, that was more like a dirty joke.

And then think about this: whatever was surfacing needn't really have been something fearful. Haven't the shrinks been telling us for almost a century that any natural urge can be blocked from its expression and twisted out of recognition? And then how could we view its coming forth with anything but fear?

"That's all very neat," you say, "but earlier you said you feared latent homosexuality. Now, it's some natural, healthy instinct you're blaming. What's it going to be next?"

And I say to you in return: Who the hell am I to say? I'm trying to unravel a whole tangled knot of rationalizations, and what it's and buts. Who knows? Maybe I'm getting myself into a worse tangle. You can probably see more clearly what's going on than I can. At least you've got some distance, and a different perspective.

It might just be this simple: what was trying to come out was me. Simply me, not the layers of bullshit that I had accepted as me and tried to live up to all my life. But the layers aren't broken so easily.

They aren't just dried, crumbly pieces of dung, no. They're dynamic forces, and they're intimately joined to what I think is me, so that when *they're* threatened, *I'm* threatened. Thus, all the fear; even though breaking free of them would be the best thing that could happen to me. But don't we all know from rude experience that growing up is a fearful thing? It has been for me, anyway.

So. Where am I going with all this sad talk of my long, slow weaning? Right back up to the Kleine Scheidegg Hotel, to my hand-shaking lunch, where else? I've told you already that that's where everything leads to and that's where everything starts. So, let's follow the lead up there and get started.

Max and I left Basel for the mountains on the day after Christmas. Jurg, the bass guitar player from Max's band, met us at the station early that morning, and we boarded the train for Interlaken and found an empty compartment. I remember later in the morning looking out the window on the rolling plain north of Bern, and getting my first sight of the Alps, snow-covered and gray under a cloudy sky. They looked like living beings, hooded, ominous, looming under the gray clouds, with none of the cheeriness that sunlight gives to snow.

Later, Herr Rossler told me that when he had been with the Swiss mountain troops during world War II, he had known men who couldn't adjust to living in the mountains, and had to be transferred to some post in the lowlands. They called the phenomenon *Bergfieber*, mountain fever, and when I heard about it, I was glad Herr Rossler hadn't told me before I got my first glimpse of the mountains, or I might have worked up a case of my own.

South of Bern, the train climbed up the valley of the Aare River into the mountains. As they rose higher and higher, the snowline dropped closer to the tracks. At Interlaken, we stepped down out of the train into the cold air of snow country, and then we carried our bags and skis over to the platform where the mountain train was loading.

Now that we were actually in the heart of the mountains, I began to feel the flatlander's shock at the magnitude of the vertical dimensions I was facing now. I had gotten in shape for skiing by walking almost every day to my classes at the University, and the Rosslers had given me a small ski instruction book in German that I had read and reread. But my heart fluttered when I saw the line of steel gear teeth down the center of the tracks of the mountain railway. A cogwheel underneath the engine engaged the teeth to pull the train, and that meant it went up grades too steep for regular wheels to pull.

We put our skis in vertical metal racks on an open flatcar, and then we climbed on and found seats. I sat by the window and watched as we pulled out of the station. The tracks crossed an open snowfield on the edge of town, and when they came to a the banks of a clear rushing stream, they turned and followed it up the abruptly rising walls of the valley. The stream rushed down with churning force over polished round rocks and boulders, and the largest boulders were capped above the waterline with cylinders of clean, white snow.

At the village of Lauterbrunnen, snow covered the rooftops and trees, and the only break in the white was the thin, black line of the tracks. With my forehead pressed against the cold glass of the window, I could see ahead to where the tracks took a turn to the left on a bridge over the stream, and then zoomed up the opposite wall of the valley at what seemed to be an impossibly steep angle.

When the train crossed the stream and began to climb, my seat tilted further and further back. I gripped the armrest of the seat and fought back a giddy impulse to shout out for someone to stop the train. I had the same trapped, desperate feeling you get after being locked into the seat of a roller coaster, and it's climbing the first long hill. But instead of taking me into a sharp, rushing drop, the train turned left again and began to traverse the valley wall, climbing higher and higher with each traverse.

Finally, we crossed over the upper lip of the valley and came to Wengen, a village of chalets, shops, and small hotels. After a short stop at the station, the train pulled out and climbed a few miles more to the head of a higher valley. This was where we were going, to the Kleine Sheidegg, a cluster of hotel buildings on either side of the tracks, with a railway station for the higher branch line of the Jungfrau Railway that took anyone who wanted to go up to the tunnel into the top of the mountain ridge that opened out to the next major valley where you could ski down into another Canton of Switzerland.

We got off the train and walked along the station platform in a biting wind. Coming around the end of the station, I looked up and saw a towering wall of snowy mountains above the hotels. Max pointed out three peaks in a row: the Eiger, Mönch, and Jungfrau. The snow and ice and the bare rock walls reaching up almost as high as the overcast didn't make me feel that this was a place to come to have fun.

The hotel buildings stood on a ridge that ran down from the foot of the Eiger and formed the head of two valleys; one, we had just climbed up in the train; the other dropped away to Grindelwald. The view back toward Wengen was blocked by the snowy lower slopes of the Lauberhorn, a nearby peak on the opposite side of the tracks from the Jungfrau. Toward Grindelwald, there was a clear view for miles down into the wide, snow-filled valley, and then across it to the peaks beyond: the Wetterhorn and the Wellhorn on the south side of the valley, and the Rötihorn and the Schwarzhorn on the north. The railway was the only motorized contact with either valley. The only other way out was by ski.

An old Swiss porter had come down to the train to meet us, and he loaded our bags on a sled and pulled it back up to the hotel. We checked in and then ate lunch in the dining room. After lunch, I took my first skiing lesson.

The teacher was a slow-talking Alpine Swiss called Charley, but I found out later that his name was really Karl, Karl Jung, yes like the famous psychologist. He told me to carry my skis down the railroad tracks on the Grindelwald side and I'd see him and the class down below. Then, he took the skiers in his class out in front of the hotel, where they put on their skis. With Charley in the lead, they skied away to the tracks and disappeared around the end of the hotel buildings.

It was snowing lightly now as I walked down the tracks, and I noticed the soft quiet of the snow all around. The only sound came from my boots crunching the snow on the railway ties. When I saw Charley, I left the tracks and headed toward him, sinking up to my knees in the snow with every step. I reached the group, and Charley skied over and took me a short distance away to a small hill.

First, Charley showed me how to put on the skis, and I remember having to take off my gloves and fumble with the cold bindings with my bare hands. I felt nervous and self-conscious with him standing right beside me watching, and the class waiting for him to come back.

When I had fastened the bindings, Charley showed me how to sidestep up the hill. At the top, he told me to face downhill and plant my ski poles to keep from sliding. Then, he told me to stand erect with my knees bent slightly. He took the same stance and then pushed off for a short, straight run down the hill. At the bottom, he looked back and shouted for me to do the same. I picked up my poles and began to slide, slowly at first, and then faster as I neared the bottom. I felt like I was whizzing down out of control, a mixed feeling of pleasure and fear.

Charley told me to sidestep back up and run down again. Then he showed me how to stop myself by opening out the back ends of the skis while keeping the tips together, and leaning forward on the inward-canted edges of the skis. He called this position the *Schneepflug*, the snowplow, and showed me how to do a snowplow turn, with his knees bent as he leaned forward over the front half of his skis which he held locked in a V from the joined ski tips back while they carried him through the arc of the turn. He explained what he was doing as he skied, shifting his weight at the end of each turn onto the opposite ski and turning slowly back the other direction.

After I tried a couple of shaky turns, Charley left me alone to practice while he worked with the rest of the class.

When the lesson was over, Charley skied over to me and said, "In a week, you will be up there." And he pointed toward the Lauberhorn. A ski lift across the tracks from the hotel pulled skiers up to a point twelve-hundred feet higher than where we stood, and the ones at the top who were starting down looked like upright, sliding ants.

"No," I said.

"Oh, yes," Charley said, with finality, and he turned out to be right.

The next morning and afternoon, my teacher was a seventy-year-old man named Hans Graf, whose silver hair and moustache, ruddy face and stocky build, made me think of Santa Claus. The morning following that, Hans sent me to the class for the next higher skill level. At the end of the day, the teacher, a tall blond Swiss named Peter, said I was good enough to make the run down to Grindelwald. That night at dinner, Max and Jurg said that they would ski down with me the next afternoon. Also, that night, I met Helena.

Every night before, we had eaten dinner in the dining room, but that evening the hotel put on a special fondue dinner in the Gaststuebli, a basement bar and restaurant with a small dance floor and bandstand, and booths around the walls.

Helena came in with her parents and her three sisters, one older and two much younger. She was wearing a close-fitting black dress with long sleeves, and a short, brown fur jacket; but I wasn't especially struck by the way she looked. If I noticed anything special about her, it was the smooth skin of her face. Her hair was brown and cut in a mid-length style that any woman, from twenty to fifty, might have worn. To me, she was just a Swiss girl who walked in with her well-to-do parents and her sisters for a boring family evening.

After dinner, Max stood up from our table and walked over to Helena's and introduced himself to her parents. Then he asked Helena's older sister, a thin blond they called Trudy, if she'd like to dance. After another shot of white wine, I stood up, followed Max's example, nodding and smiling to the parents while I introduced myself, and then I asked Helena to dance. She took off the fur jacket and slid out of the booth, and maybe then it was that I first noticed the attractive round curves of her figure. I must have felt them while we were dancing, because I remember wondering if she could feel the building evidence of my growing attraction for her.

I don't know if we talked during that first dance, but as the evening went on and we danced again, I found out that Helena went to a French school in Lausanne and was spending the last week of holidays skiing with her family. Like Max and Jurg, she would be leaving on New Year's Day.

That night, the parents took the two younger girls and left Helena and Trudy in the Gaststuebli. Max and Jurg and I moved to their booth, and Max ordered a carafe of white wine. Sometime during the evening, Max told the sisters that I was making my first run to Grindelwald the next afternoon.

"Oh," Helena said, "what class are you in?"

"The second."

"I am, too. I've never skied down to Grindelwald, either. Can I come, too?"

"Sure," I said, "but we ought to ask Max to see if he minds taking two beginners."

Max said it was all right with him, and Trudy said she would come along, too. When the band stopped playing, we said good night, and I walked back through the cold night to the hotel room with Max and Jurg, looking forward to the next afternoon's skiing with Helena. After a night of dancing and talking with her, I no longer felt the indifference I had when she first walked into the room.

It turned out that Helena was an expert skier, and it was her idea of a joke to pass herself off as a beginner. When we started out the next day for Grindelwald, she shot down the slope from the tracks, leaving a smooth, curving trail in the snowfield where Charley had given me my first lesson.

She stopped at the edge of the field and waited while I snowplowed down through the powder. That's the way it went for the rest of the run down: the four of them would race down and then hold up and wait for me to flounder my way down to them.

Later, she told me that she was amazed that I wasn't embarrassed to ski with them, being such a rank beginner. I told her the physical effort quickly took my mind off my punctured pride, and somehow, it didn't even bother me that I had been the butt of her joke. Actually, it made her seem deeper, more mysterious, and then, I always had liked women who stung me.

Once, during the run to Grindelwald, Helena told me I wasn't doing bad for only four days of ski lessons. "I've been skiing since I was a little girl," she said. "My father taught me. He'd hold me between his skis on my little skis."

"If you want to, I'd let you give me a lesson like that," I said.

"No," she said, "I don't want to." But she laughed as she turned and skied away.

At Grindelwald, we had a drink in the café near the station, and on the train back up, Helena and I sat together. Back up on the mountain, we got off the train and walked through the dark toward the lights of the hotel. We stopped in the light below the large windows of the lobby, and I asked her to meet me in the Gaststuebli after dinner. She smiled and said she would, and then she climbed the steps and went into the hotel.

My memory of the next few days isn't clear, but I know that Helena and I met in the Gaststuebli every night and drank wine and danced until the band stopped playing. Then, we'd hang around the lobby after everyone else had gone to their rooms, and we'd make out for a few minutes before she went upstairs. Then, I'd walk alone down across the tracks to the annex.

One of those nights was clear and moonlit, and when I got to the room, Max and Jurg were putting on their ski boots for a moonlight run on the Lauberhorn.

"Are you drunk?" I asked Max.

"No, Wally," he said, "it's the moonlight."

"How will you get up without the lift?"

"We'll herringbone up the lift path," Jurg said, "and sidestep where it's steep."

I went out and watched them slide off in the moonlight, poling their way toward the lift. At first, I could hear them talking and laughing as they climbed, but soon their voices were muffled by the snow. I couldn't see them very well, either, just the movement of dark forms against the snow, or a thin flash of moonlight on a chrome pole. Then, I lost sight of them altogether, and to keep warm, I began to stamp around in the snow.

Down in the valley, the lights of Grindelwald were shining, and up in the hotel one window glowed orange with the light from the room striking the window shade. I wondered if that was Helena's room. Then, I heard a faint call from Max and looked back up at the Lauberhorn. At first, I couldn't see anything, but then movement on the lower slopes caught my eye and I heard Max laughing. Then, I saw the two dark figures, turning back and forth down the slope. They straightened out on the flat between me and the lift and glided up to where I stood.

So, it sounds nice, doesn't it? My little ski idyll in the mountains; drinking and dancing with Helena; watching my wild young friends ski in the moonlight. But it wasn't to last undisturbed much longer.

Helena and I skied together once more, on New Year's Eve Day, this time down the valley to Wengen. When we left the hotel after lunch, the sky was clear. The snow of the peaks stood out against the blue sky, and the fir trees in the valley made green triangles against the sunlit snow. We skied down, facing the afternoon sun, and much of the run wound between stands of tall, dark firs. From time to time, the sound of yodeling came up through the trees from the trail below.

I was skiing faster than on the run to Grindelwald, so we made the shorter trip to Wengen quickly and had a long wait for the next train back up the mountain. We left our skis at the Wengen station and walked up the snow-filled street to a small disco.

Inside, it was crowded and warm, and a large fire burned in an open fireplace. We sat at a small table and watched the pack of skiers on the dance floor. A girl came and took our order for drinks, and when she brought them, we sat and drank without talking since we couldn't hear each other without shouting over the music.

When we left the disco to catch the train back up to the Kleine Scheidegg, it was dark outside, and the snow in the street had frozen in hard ruts. We picked up our skis at the station and waited beside the tracks for the train. When it pulled up, we fastened our skis into the racks on the flatcar and crowded onto a car with the other skiers. There weren't enough seats to go around, so I sat in an aisle seat, and Helena sat on my lap.

Max climbed on our car, and when he saw us, he came and stood near us in the aisle. His face was flushed with wine and the cold, and soon he began to sing. First, he sang in English, "She'll be comin' 'round the mountain," and the few of us who knew the words joined in. Then, he switched to German songs, and everyone sang with him. Some of the Alpine-Swiss yodeled in the songs that called for it.

Once again, I wondered if Helena could feel that I was turned on. I thought she must, because I could feel the separate cheeks of her bottom through the tight nylon ski pants she wore. From time to time in the singing, she's smile at me and lean her shoulder into my chest, and I'd hug her close. I knew she was leaving the next day, and I kept thinking of how I was going to miss her.

New Year's Eve was a special event at the hotel. Everyone was expected to *dress* for dinner. Max and Jurg and I wore dinner jackets, and the women all came in long gowns. On the dining tables, each place setting contained a party hat and a paper horn, and clear cellophane packs of rolled colored paper streamers. When we sat down, Max and Jurg put on the hats and broke open the streamers. Max took one of the rolls and threw it over the people at the next table. Then, the other guests began to throw the rolled streamers in raveling arches across the room, and soon the room was crisscrossed with a web of colored paper lines.

After dinner, we went down to the Gaststuebli and sat at a booth with Helena and Trudy. Max and I ordered white wine in liter carafes and kept them coming, one after the other. Helena and I danced every dance, mainly to be able to hold each other, and I can remember walking off the floor under the approving glances of the older people ("What a *lovely* young couple!") with the dizzy, almost nauseous feeling of interrupted, hot arousal in a public place.

Midnight comes back with all the horn-blowing and kissing and more colored paper streamers and Helena pressed against me for a long kiss on the dance floor. My next memory is of the members of the band, three Germans from Hamburg, coming to our booth for a glass of wine after they had finished playing. And then everyone who was leaving the next day said goodbye and went to their rooms.

My next memory is of holding Helena as she leaned against the wall in one of the rooms off the front hall. While we kissed, I slowly inched up her dress, expecting her to stop me. But she didn't, and I soon realized she welcomed any move my hands were making, so I reached under her dress with both hands and slipped them down into the back of her panties, caressing the fine, round cheeks I had admired all week outlined so well in her tight ski pants.

And now, after all these years, I can still remember through the memory-shroud of wine, the familiar, delicious combination of silky panties and warm, smooth skin, but not much else. I know that we didn't have sex, but I don't know how long we stood there. The next thing I knew, it was morning, and I was in my bed in the annex with an awful feeling of sickness and dread.

Now, *now* you can see why I felt so awful. I had done it again, hadn't I? Gotten so drunk I had forgotten parts of the evening, just like the morning I woke up in jail. This time, though, the physical symptoms felt even worse. My head was roaring with pain and swimming in dizzy circles, and my stomach churned with nausea. Pangs of fear and guilt shot through my chest when I thought of the night before and all the wine I drank. So, you can see why the thought of getting up from the safety of the warm sheets and striking out into the cold air didn't fill me with delight.

Then, when Max told me what time it was, and I realized I had missed skiing that morning, can you understand why I writhed with guilt under the covers? I hadn't had any work for months, so I hadn't earned a vacation. In fact, since Herr Rossler was paying my way at the hotel, I really felt obligated to give him his money's worth by taking advantage of every opportunity to improve my skiing. Skiing was my work, the way I could earn my keep, and that morning I hadn't earned it. Now, Herr Rossler was coming up this afternoon. What return would I have to show for his investment but a hangover that had caused me to miss work?

Then, there were the jokes from Max and Jurg about where I'd been early that morning. No wonder I moaned. The thought of someone catching Helena and me in the lobby with her dress hiked up around her waist made me want to pull the covers up over my head and never come out. And now that you know the whole story of what went on between me and Frau Rossler over sex, you can understand my panic flutters of guilt and shame: she had asked me not to bring sex into her house. I was their guest at the hotel, so in a way, it *was* their house. I had brought sex into the hotel, hadn't I? Therefore, I had brought it into her house; and now she was on her way up on the afternoon train.

"Absurd," you say. That's right, it was absurd, and I probably knew it at the time; but the thing about it is, knowing that didn't make me feel any less guilty. In fact, the more absurd I knew my guilty fear to be, the stronger it grew.

And then, when Max and Jurg and I were finally dressed and had walked to the hotel, it didn't help me to see the guests who'd skied that morning coming in for lunch with the healthy glow of exercise and cold air on their laughing faces. What would they have thought of me if they'd known I'd just dragged my polluted body out of the sack? And what was even worse, what would they have thought of what I'd been doing up until I hit the sack--standing right in the lobby mauling a nice young Swiss girl, while her parents were sleeping just a floor or two away in the same building?

So, you can see I felt judged even before I went into the dining room, but it helped to be with Max and Jurg, belonging to a group, being able to hide in the herd, even such a small one. But then they left me all alone in that roomful of strangers, and I began to shrivel under the imagined, stern gaze of a higher social jury. I felt naked — I had no one to hide behind now. And talk about not belonging. Just sitting there alone with all those members of a wealthy, more sophisticated social class than the one I was used to, gave me the final outward shove. I didn't belong there. I had climbed too high. Wasn't Frau Rossler to say later that day that my shaking hands were a symptom of altitude sickness? Well, she was right, but it was an altitude of a different kind.

Then, once the shaking started, it presented a new struggle in itself. Regardless of what I was hiding that caused the shame and fear, the fear itself was something to hide; the very fact that I was afraid caused me shame.

And now, it comes to me as a shock that in all this talk of fear and remorse and shame and everything I had to hide, the only aspect that was visible to the world, the only thing that anyone could possibly have noticed, was my inability to bring a spoonful of sherbet the twelve inches from a goblet to my mouth without my hand shaking. And for that, I came to believe it was necessary to throw my life away.

* * *

8

This morning the muffled roar of the neighbor's truck woke me. I reached down for the flashlight and shone it on the clock. Five-twenty. Good. The noisy bastard did me a favor for a change. Christ, I've let them spoil my life. I haven't seen them face to face for over a month, but I've kept them in my thoughts—I've even had long, drawn-out arguments with them, all in imagination.

Will I ever grow out of this morbid sensitivity? Why do I have to be so open to every remark, every look I think's directed at me? Why do I have to rip open my rib cage and ask every passing stranger to prod my throbbing heart, tear it with their nails, stub out their cigarette butts on it.

Ah, Al, where did you go? Before you left, it was so quiet next door. The only sounds you made were when you called your little foo-foo dog, Killer, to take him for a walk. But now, there's a whole menagerie: an old, broken-down Weimaraner bitch, a yowling Siamese cat named Sebastian, and a large, white, parrot-like bird that shrieks when the dog barks, all locked up together in that shack that's no bigger than our little hovel.

And if that wasn't enough, the woman had a cousin who bunked in with them for a while, and *he* had a dog, too. The cousin wore a fu manchu moustache and had long hair that hung down in sausage curls, and he called his dog, Reefer.

Now he's gone, but I heard the woman telling a friend to come in and see the iguana they brought back with them from Mexico. Can you imagine the smells that all that variety of animal crap must work up over there? Wait till summer, then I won't have to imagine it.

Then the noise will stoke up again with all the windows open, their music, their cheap friends, talking at the top of their lungs, laughing like mad at nothing, anything, anything to keep away the sad knowledge of their empty lives.

Since they've been back from Mexico, though, they've been more careful about the noise, but I still hear them. They shoot their mouths off when they're coming and going, or when a friend passes by. Yesterday, I heard her tell someone about the iguana, and her squawking, raucous voice broadcast the knowledge to the world, "I'm not workin' anymore, I'm just doin' my art."

That's right, she claims to be an *artist*; she even has a "studio" in the back of a house at the end of 15th Street, but I don't know when she makes the time to art. She's got small, black eyes that she wears too much makeup on, and a big, fat ass that she keeps stuffed into too-tight jeans, but that's the only evidence I can see of any painting or sculpting going on over there. Mainly, she sits on that ass and shouts from the porch at anyone who'll listen.

But what was I doing to myself, lying in bed, letting the neighbors get me down, keep me down? I had to get up, get moving. This was frustration, death, to lie there when I should be writing. I slid out slowly so I wouldn't wake Ellie, and I did my usual morning quick-dress routine in the orange glow of the electric heater. Sweatshirt, sweatpants, watch cap, gloves, wool socks.

When I was dressed, I padded to the back door and opened it and looked up to the east to see if the morning star was visible. Yes, fat and bright, no clouds in the sky, and no light yet from the sun.

Our cat, Rupert, galloped around the corner of the house, meowing his growling, complaining, hungry-morning meow. I stepped out on the small piece of man-made marble and faced the east to do my circling ceremony while Rupert rubbed against my legs.

First a step to the East, to the morning star, and I mumble, "Help me, Wakan Tanka, that my people may live. Help me with the wisdom and light of the morning star."

I step back to the center, always returning to the center, to the Earth, then turn clockwise to the South and take a step. "Help me, Wakan Tanka, with the light that grows from the South, the South whence life comes. Give me life and let me live it."

Back to the center, then a turn and a step to the West, where the water beings live. "Help me, Wakan Tanka, that my people may live. Bring me water, water of the spirit to dissolve all dead forms that bind my life."

Back to the center and turn to the North, where the thunder beings live. "Let them blow their cold winds down and make us strong."

Then back to the center and look to the sky, ask all the beings that fly to give us their wisdom.

Finally, down to the Earth, the place from which all things come and to which they return.

I glanced up quickly at the second-story windows that look down over our back fence. Was anyone watching? What would people do if they saw me revolving at my back door, chanting under my breath? Who knows? Maybe someone's up there now, doing their own spins and chants.

Back in the kitchen, I took a can of frozen orange juice from the freezer, opened it, and plopped the gooey stuff in Ellie's ancient blender. I was thinking about where I learned the ceremony, from a little book called *The Sacred Pipe: Black Elk's Account of the Seven Rites of the Oglala Sioux.* My Jungian therapist gave it to me and told me I might use the rite called Hanblecheyapi, crying for a vision. I read the book, and the next time I saw him, I told him I was going to the desert to try the Hanblecheyapi; but I was afraid I might get out there and actually have a vision, actually see something at night.

"Who knows?" he said, "You might."

Now, I just noticed that while I was thinking about my therapist, I went to the fridge and got the eggs and broke two into the blender with the orange juice. I was supposed to put the eggs into Ellie's glass of juice, not in the whole batch. *She's* the one we're force-feeding so the little being that's growing in her will come out happy, strong, and healthy, not me. I took a breath and looked around me. "Watch where you are," I said to myself, "All these thoughts distract you. You might get a hand blended in with the orange juice and eggs. *Be here now. Be here now.*"

And now, sitting at the desk in this dark, cold house, writing before Ellie wakes, it occurs to me that someone out there must be wondering, "What is it with this guy? I thought all this circular analysis was supposed to get him back on track, to start him on the way to someplace real, but he's lucky to make it out of his kitchen in one piece. What's the good of all the analytical, anal-clinical circling if he never gets anywhere? What's he trying to prove? That the over-examined life's not worth living?"

Well, all right, then. That attitude is understandable. I mean, now that all the pieces of this large, circular puzzle have fallen into place (or now that I've forced them in place, whittling a few edges to make them fit), shouldn't I feel some kind of resolution of my problems? When I finished the page about the Kleine Scheidegg, didn't I sit for a moment, trembling with anticipation? Didn't I stand up and draw a breath of joy, rush to the front door and wrench it open, jump out onto the slanting porch that's being levered up year-by-year by the cypress tree that grows against it, bounce down the resilient, root-raised steps, shrieking out my liberation to the world, "I'm *free*! I'm *free*!"?

No?

What, then?

Well...well....You want too much, that's what! Look, haven't you ever had a scab you picked at, even though there was always someone around who told you not to? You know how it feels when the scab is dry and hard, and it shrinks and pulls the skin tight on either side, and where the skin is tightest, the edge of the scab breaks loose a little and lifts, letting a tiny drop of yellow liquid squeeze out? And then, even though it hurts, you scratch at that lifted edge with a fingernail, pulling, worrying, rolling back the scab, painfully, bit-by-bit, until finally your frayed nerves can't take it any longer, and you have to finish off the job with a quick jerk that sets the sore bleeding again. You know how that is, don't you?

Well, then, maybe that's all I'm doing here, scratching at a scab, and didn't our mothers all tell us that the longer we scratch, the harder it is to heal? Maybe the only hope I can offer myself (and you) is this: if I keep scratching long enough, my fingers will finally tire.

I said I was going to write down what happened to me that year. I've made a good start; now I have to finish. It may just be that simple. And then, if I find my fingers are ready to move again, ready to pick guitar strings instead of scabs, to open new worlds instead of old wounds, then all right, all right. But don't you rush me.

Now, somewhere back along the way, I told you that everything leads to the lunch on the Kleine Scheidegg, and everything starts there. It was the Great Divide of my life, and what does *Scheidegg* mean in German if not a *divide*? Before that New Year's Day on the Kleine Scheidegg, I lived the common, smoothly flowing existence of a young man on his way up. After, it seems that I haven't performed a single act without questioning whether or not I could get through it without risking another attack of hand-shaking fear. And yet, I know that's an exaggeration.

There have been stretches of time when I haven't feared the fear. In fact, after the ski run down to Grindelwald and the reassuring response from the Rosslers that night at dinner, I pretty much forgot about what had happened at lunch. That strikes me now as impossible, but it's true. It wasn't until the Saturday evening I was typing up the Rotary speech that the fear hit me again, and then I went round and round over the same fearful ground. Would my hands shake at the Rotary luncheons?

What made it even worse was the fact that I had no frame of reference for what was happening–there was nothing in my experience that would help me make sense of it. It just came across as irrational fear. No, actually, there was one idea that I ran across that seemed to apply, but it only promised worse things yet to come. I found it in *Advertisements for Myself*, and it went something like this: whenever you face someone in a conflict, you either win or you get faced down. If you win, you gain access to power for further conflicts. If you get faced down, you lose power. In other words, each defeat in life makes you more defeatable, and that's the part I fastened on, because after the lunch, I imagined myself in the defeated role.

But even before the speeches, I had to risk defeat, in a class at the university. It was a German class for foreign students taught by Frau Milena von Eckhardt, a middle-aged actress. She was short and plump, and she wore her gray hair cropped close to her head, but she was still attractive, and I could tell she had been beautiful when she was young. That memory of beauty, and the fact that I saw her once at the Komödie, playing a role in Durrenmatt's, *Der Meteor*, made me want to get to know her better. So, one day after class I talked to her about practicing my Rotary speech in front of the class. She liked the idea.

Thinking back on it now, I wonder why I don't have any memory of dread at talking to the class, and I realize, again with surprise, that I hadn't yet generalized the fear of my hands' shaking to every situation where I'd have to perform in public. Also, it was a low-key group of only seven or eight foreign students, and I was on easy speaking terms with all of them.

On the day I was to speak, Frau von Eckhardt told the class what I was going to do, and then she sat down in the front row of the classroom. I stepped up on the speaker's platform and put my papers on the lectern. I began to read, and then, even though I knew the students and Frau von Eckhardt, and though I felt no special threat from any one of them, here came the fear, just like at the Kleine Scheidegg. My heart pounded, my hands shook, and my chest tightened up so tight I couldn't breathe.

I stopped reading and stood there looking down at the papers with a little smile on my face. Now, what was that smile all about? It was the same one I would smile the day in the hallway when the two students mocked the way I walked. It was as if I were saying to the world, "Now look at this; isn't this silly? I'm cracking up and I haven't the slightest idea what to do about it." But why smile? Did I really think it was funny that something inside me was producing fear in greater intensity than I'd ever experienced?

No. I was trying my best not to show the fear, not to embarrass anyone, so I kept up that fastidious, smiling front when I was choking inside. What I really felt like doing was letting my trembling knees buckle and drop me to the floor, where I could ball up with my arms clutched around my stomach and roll, groaning with fear. Instead, I just stood there, holding it all back behind that little smile.

I looked up at Frau von Eckhardt and mumbled, "*Entshuldiqen.*" Excuse me.

"What's the matter?" she asked in German, "Are you afraid?"

"Yes," I said.

"Sit down there," she said, pointing to a desk on the platform.

I sat down, bringing my speech with me. By the time I had arranged the pages in front of me, my heart had slowed down and my breathing eased, so I started reading where I had left off. Soon, the fear passed, and I stood back up and finished the speech at the lectern. When I sat down, I remember thinking, "What if the fear comes when I stand up in front of the Rotary Club, and there's no Frau von Eckhardt to come to the rescue?"

After class, I stopped to talk to Frau von Eckhardt. Her response to my fear had been so quick and effective, I thought she might know some magic I could use to keep from freaking out the next time I had to speak. When I asked her, she said she'd give me the name and address of her doctor, and he could prescribe some tranquilizers for me.

Tranquilizers! Not *me*. If I started taking tranquilizers, that would mean something really *was* wrong with me, that I really *was* loony or on the way down the road to loonyhood and drug dependency.

"I thought you might know something I could do to keep from having the fear," I said.

"No," she said, "but these will help when it comes."

"Thanks, but I think I'd like to try something else first."

"All right, but don't worry yourself too much over it. It's just *Lampenfieber.*"

Lampfever? I translated what I thought it was in English.

I didn't get what she meant by that, so I asked her what it was. She said it was the anxiety actors and actresses get before going on stage. Oh, stage fright, stage-lamp fever. Yes, nothing to worry about; everyone gets it.

Curious, isn't it, how everyone had such a lighthearted explanation for my dark fear? Frau Rossler had said it was caused by the altitude, Herr Rossler, the white wine, now Frau von Eckhardt cast her vote for nothing more than stage fright.

"*LOOK!*" I wanted to bellow at them, "It's not that simple. I'm *SCARED*, and I don't want to be scared, and what's worse, I don't even have a good reason to be scared." And even though I smiled when the fear had hit me, I knew this wasn't anything to smile at—this was very serious business.

My whole future was at stake, my sanity, couldn't they see that? No, they couldn't. From where they were, it just didn't look that bad. How could they know I was creating a life and death situation out of feeling anxious in front of strangers? How could they know that, rain or shine, I carried my own portable rain cloud to darken my world? I didn't even know it myself, for at the time, I was too much in it to imagine things any other way.

So, I began in earnest to dread the situations in which I'd feel fear, and to multiply them as I went along. First, I discovered that sitting alone with a hangover in a luxury hotel dining room would freak me out; then, pronouncing Russian words in front of a class of students; and next, I had to make speeches at Rotary Clubs.

Oh, Jesus, what bleak, sleepless nights and barren, forlorn days I suffered over those speeches--what loose bowels, what eruptions of zits and fever blisters! After the idea came of what might happen to me in front of the Rotarians, it turned into an evil merry-go-round that all my thoughts rode over and over again.

Finally, I had to tell someone, and since I was afraid to see a shrink about it, I decided to confide in Frau Rossler. She already knew what had happened at lunch on New Year's Day, so it wasn't a very big step to tell her what had happened since.

Well, she tried her best to help, and I have to say she was a very good listener, but what could she do, what could she say? She couldn't go and give the speeches in my place, could she, and that's about the only thing that would have done any good. But she tried. She recommended the "nerve drops" to keep me calm during the speeches.

Herr Rossler, when we let him in on the problem, said he used the drops once a year when he had to pass his annual army marksmanship test with the pistol. He said without the drops, his hand trembled a little, but with them, his hand was steady as a rock, and he had held his fist out in front of him, index finger pointing toward an imaginary target.

When I walked down to Neuwilerplatz to buy the drops, I nervously rehearsed what I was going to say in German, so that by the time I got to the foot of the hill and crossed the street to the drugstore, my heart was pounding almost as hard as it had in Frau von Eckhardt's class. Still, I managed to stammer out what I needed to the lady behind the counter, and then I took the drops back up to the Rosslers'.

That afternoon I tried out the drops, but I couldn't tell if they worked, because right then, I didn't have a fear situation to test them in. All I noticed was a feeling of drowsiness, so I was left in doubt as to what would happen when I had to stand up and actually give a speech.

Frau Rossler had told me she knew of a remedy for stage fright other than the drops. I had perked up at that and listened hopefully for what she would have to say. She told me to take ten deep breaths just before I had to get up to speak. Just that? Take ten breaths? *That* was a letdown. It didn't sound to me like it would help much, but I planned to try it anyway.

Herr Rossler had a different remedy. He said that when he had to address a crowd, as he did every Monday of that year as president of the Basel Rotary Club, he repeated a formula in his head that kept him from feeling scared. Once again, I felt a thrill of hope. What was the formula?

"They can lick my ass," he said in German.

They can *lick* my *ass*? My God, if I thought something like that, it would make things even worse! A large part of my problem was the feeling of strangeness and alienation from the people around me. If I said something like that, even to myself, it would place me even further in opposition to the world, and that was the last thing I wanted. No, I'd stay with the drops and the deep breaths, and leave the insults alone.

Someone else I told my troubles to was Kaspar Heer, the medical student I had met at the university and slowly got to be friends with. Do you remember Kaspar? He's the one I told I was neurotic, but he disagreed and looked up the term in his medical dictionary and read me the symptoms to show me I was wrong. But his rational argument didn't help much, except to reassure me that I didn't fit the handbook definition of a neurotic. So, in the final analysis, it was up to me to handle it alone. And that's generally the way things go, isn't it?

Still, I kept trying to figure out ways to reduce the anxiety, and after Frau von Eckhardt's class, I had the lucky idea that I could show slides with my speech. That way I could stand in darkness at the back of the room, while the slide screen would be at the front to take all those eyes off me. The speech was about my home area of South Louisiana and the city of Baton Rouge, so I wrote to the president of the Rotary Club there and asked him if he could send me some slides showing the industry and life of Louisiana.

I sweated out the time before the slides arrived, because the date for my first speech had already been set, but they got there in time for me to rewrite the speech to fit them. My main worry now was that the people at the Olten Rotary Club, where I was to make my first speech, might forget to arrange for a slide projector.

And I worried plenty, sweating out the agony of anticipation until the day of the first speech came. And come it did, as dreaded days do come, with an amazing kind of dragging speed, rushing slowly toward us.

Sometimes I think my memory has invented the details of that morning, using a whole pile of material from subsequent mornings of dread before speeches (and Marine training, and new jobs, and...and...and...). But some are so specific, they must belong to that first day: Frau Rossler at breakfast with a pot of her nerve tea, then standing at the front door reminding me about the ten deep breaths and checking my little airline flight-bag to make sure I had everything I needed: the speech, the slides, the nerve drops and something extra I'd thought of, a book to read on the train to take my mind off the speech.

I have vivid memories of earlier in the morning, but they're the ones that could be from any number of mornings, waking before daylight and checking the alarm clock on the headboard, a small, folding travel-clock with a tan leather case and luminous, gold hands, waking and seeing I still had hours before I had to get up, but not being able to go back to sleep. Then getting up and going into the bathroom, squinting from the white light that stabbed at my eyes from every direction, reflecting off the bright, white tiles of the walls and floor, pissing, and walking back to the medicine cabinet over the lavatory in my own room where I kept the nerve drops.

I can still see the small, brown bottle with its dropper squeeze-top, and the off-white label's brown lettering, and I remember holding it in my hand while I read the directions, so many drops every four hours, then unscrewing the cap, squeezing the drops into a glass of water, downing the cloudy mixture, and crawling back in bed. Next, the clock would be ringing, and I'd fight back up sluggishly, shower, and drink another dose of the drops, even though it hadn't been four hours since the first, because I didn't want to risk their wearing off between doses.

And the train rides, too, merge in memory; five of them to five of the six speeches I gave, but the first, to Olten, stands out. I remember I sat in a window seat in a compartment that I had all to myself. During much of the southeastern journey, the sun was shining in through my window, but it gave me little comfort. In fact, it seemed somehow wrong for the situation, almost unfair, that the sun was shining down out of a bright, blue sky, bringing out the rich green of the winter crops and stands of pines and firs in the fields as the train sped by. I thought of all the people who must have been uplifted by the day, not a care in the world, while I was on my way to what I feared was going to be my doom.

I took out the book I'd brought to read, *The Drama of the Absurd*. I opened the book to a chapter called, "The Curable and the Uncurable," about Arthur Adamov, and it gave me a feeling of reassurance to read that he had suffered such emotional turmoil as a young man. After all, hadn't he gone on to become an internationally known playwright? Didn't that hold out some promise of hope for me?

But then I read that Adamov had had problems with sex during that time, with sexual impotence, and he would even go to prostitutes and reveal his impotence to them and ask them to humiliate him for it. *Sexual impotence!*

The words alone were enough to make me weaken down there with doubts of my manhood. And with a habit I was forming of identifying with every fear or phobia I read about, I asked myself if this was next in line. Would I now begin to worry about whether or not I would be able to get it up at the crucial moment? I closed the book and put it back in my flight-bag, and after that, I have no more memories of the trip.

The next thing I remember is being shown into an office of a printing company to meet Herr Doctor Eugen Meyer, whose name I wouldn't remember, but I still have it on a white card along with the name of the printing company, Verlag Otto Walter; and a few, blue, felt-tip lines that sketch out the Olten station, the Aare River (with arrows showing the direction of flow), a bridge across it, and a long arrow that starts at the station, crosses the bridge, and turns downstream, evidently the line of march I took to reach Herr Doctor Meyer, the director of Verlag Otto Walter.

I think the reason my memories are so sketchy at this point is that they were cleared out by the high voltage anxiety juicing through me during the last couple of hours before the speech. My whole nervous system was overloaded with horrifying rehearsals of the doom to be mine, and I only functioned consciously in the present in short snatches and fragments, just enough to keep me moving and responding to the people who made the greatest demands on my attention.

Someone took me on a tour of the Verlag Otto Walter, but whoever it was is nameless, faceless, and sexless, a wraith I know existed, because I know I had the tour–I say so in one of the reports I wrote to Rotary International, and I do remember talking for a moment to a press foreman, a Yugoslav in a light-green worker's smock. We stood beside a stopped printing press, and I marveled that the rolls of printed paper on the press would soon become the pages of the famous German magazine, *Die Stern*, and here it was being printed in Olten, Switzerland!

Next, Doktor Meyer and I are walking back upstream on the tree-lined street beside the Aare, and he's telling me about the covered wooden bridge that crosses the river above the station. He said it was built in1803 to replace one just like it that dated from the Middle Ages but was burned by Napoleon's troops in 1798. When we reached the bridge, we turned away from it onto the street that crossed the bridge into the heart of the old town. At the town's center, we passed a square tower that Doktor Meyer called the Stadtsturm, the City Tower, all that was left standing of a medieval church.

Our final destination, the restaurant where the Rotary Club met, was housed in a two-story, Black Forest style building with white stucco walls divided by black beams into squares and triangles.

Doktor Meyer and I went around to the side and climbed up a set of stairs to a second-story entrance, and from that point on, everything that happened at the luncheon stuck in my memory in vivid detail.

Just inside the door, an entrance hallway led into a large conference room. Along the left hand wall, a long table with a white tablecloth was set with hors d'oeuvres and rows of glasses of white wine in trays of crushed ice.

Men wearing dark, three-piece suits stood in small groups in the hall, holding wine glasses from the table and talking and laughing. Wine at lunch? Maybe I should have a shot. But no; that would be drinking because I needed it, and I was afraid to do that, and besides, for me that would be drinking on the job.

Doktor Meyer began to introduce me to the Rotarians, and I remember finding it almost impossible to look all those strangers in the face and mumble in German the false pleasantries of meeting. We moved through the groups of men out into the large room where more of the long tables with white tablecloths had been placed end-to-end, forming a large "U". Behind the closed end of the U, I saw with a catch in my heart, a speaker's lectern with a small, goose-necked lamp on it. The way I felt, that lectern might as well have been a gallows.

Just then, a short man in a sports coat and bow tie broke away from one of the groups across the room and strode over to us.

He introduced himself as Herr Doktor Tchumi, the program president of the club. I asked him if he had arranged the slide projector, and he said, "Yes, yes. We've got everything you need." He took me over to a small card table with a slide projector on it. A screen with tripod legs stood beside the table. Herr Tchumi said I could go ahead and load the projector now, and we'd put it all in place after lunch. I thanked him, and he left me alone at the table.

Now, at this point, I didn't have much hope that I'd really be able to make the speech. My heart had stepped up its tempo, and my hands were already trembling, and ever since Doktor Meyer had walked in with me and closed the door behind us, I had begun to feel trapped. I didn't think I could handle the fear and still speak, but I felt powerless to do anything to get away. So, even though I knew I wasn't going to make it, I went through the motions of putting the slides into the cassette of the projector, standing all the while with my back to the men in the room so they couldn't see my shaking hands.

By the time I'd finished, the Rotarians were moving to the take their seats around the big U of tables.

Herr Tchumi beckoned to me from the base of the U, and I went and sat beside him. Avoiding the eyes in the room, I looked down at the table and saw a small white card with my name on it, lying above my plate. Several waitresses were already at work bringing the soup course, but food was the last thing I wanted, especially soup. How would I have ever been able to get a spoonful of soup to my mouth without splashing half of it on my tie? When the waitress came to me with a bowl, I told her no thanks.

The man on the other side of me asked me a couple of polite questions that I don't remember, and I don't even remember what his face looked like, but I can still see his hands as he broke the pieces of French bread and spooned up the soup. They were large hands, strong and steady, and they went about getting the soup and bread to the man's mouth in a smooth, businesslike manner, without any hesitations or second thoughts or trembling strain, just unconsciously taking care of business. That man was sitting elbow to elbow with me, but I felt he was a world away. He was in the real world, eating a pleasant lunch among friends and business associates, but I...I was cut off, isolated, sitting inside an invisible, impenetrable bubble of fear.

And just as sunshine had seemed all wrong for the day, it felt absurd that this room was filled with the hubbub of clinking china and silver, of busy waitresses and friendly talk and laughter.

And now the fear began to rise up me in slow waves. This was it: this was the day I'd dreaded every day for two months. Now, in the time it would take for these men to finish their lunch, I would have to stand up and...and...my heart started to pound. I felt short of breath, and I began to breathe against the feeling. A prickly, cold sensation crawled up from my stomach, up through my chest and shoulders and the back of my neck, up and over my scalp.

There was a brackish, metallic taste in my mouth, and my face felt drained of blood. I looked to see if anyone noticed, but no, they just went on eating and talking, while I sat there in the strangest world I'd ever been in. And yet we were all sitting in the same room.

Then I knew I couldn't do it. Not only could I not make the speech, I couldn't go on living, because one led eventually to the other. These men would see me fail, then the world would know, and I'd never be able to show my face again anywhere. I was finished. So, what was the point? I realized I had to get out of there! In a flash, it came to me what to do: ask them where the bathroom was and then go lock myself in until the coast was clear. All right, get going! Say something! But I just sat there, unable to move.

When the waitress came with the next course, I held my hand up and refused the food with a gesture. Herr Tchumi noticed it and said in German, "Aren't you eating anything?"

"No," I answered.

"What's the matter? Are you afraid?"

"Yes," I said, embarrassed to admit it, but at the same time, glad to be able to tell someone.

"Do you drink wine?"

"Yes."

"Wine!" he shouted, clapping me on the shoulder. "*Wein, Mensch! Wein!*" He waved a waitress over and asked her to bring a carafe of red wine. When she came back with it, he told her to bring me the main course. Then he poured me a glass of the red wine and said, "*Prost!*" raising his own glass.

"*Prost,*" I said, and I drank down half the glass. Herr Tchumi filled my glass again, and I took another big slug of the wine. The warmth of the wine quickly spread through me, and my heart began to slow down. When the food came, I actually felt hungry, and Herr Tchumi poured me another glass of wine to go with the food. I don't remember *what* I ate, just *that* I ate and I drank the wine.

Giving the speech was an anti-climax after the attack of fear I had suffered during the meal. I set up the screen at the open end of the U of tables, and I stood behind the lectern at the base of the U.

The room was dark except for the shaded lamp that shone down on the typed pages of my speech.

Just as I had planned, the slides took the men's attention off me. When I started to read, my heart pounded, but I felt it through a layer of insulation the wine had laid down. My little smile came, but I kept on reading, and my heartbeats were soon back to normal.

After I finished, Herr Tchumi said the members would like to have a question-and-answer period. I surprised myself by agreeing without feeling much reluctance. In fact, I was feeling pretty high by then, with the wine and the exhilaration of having finished the speech.

Only one of the questions stays with me: one of the Rotarians asked me how long I'd studied German before coming to Switzerland. I told him I'd taken an intensive course my final year at Vanderbilt, and then the past summer, I'd attended a six-week intensive session at a language institute in Salzburg.

He said he found it almost impossible that I could have learned so much German in so little time. A tense silence fell over the room.

"You said it," I answered in German, "*Almost* impossible." The silence broke in waves of laughter that washed up over me, replacing the waves of fear I'd felt earlier. I remember that the man laughed, too, and raised his arms in a gesture that seemed to say, "I asked for that one."

Cocky me. I had made it through the speech, and through a question-and-answer period in German, and now I was cracking jokes in German, too.

After the meeting was over, I had some time to kill before my train, so Herr Tchumi took me to his office in a square, modern building several blocks from the restaurant. It was a dentist's office in a clinic he shared with several other dentists, including his father. He showed me the father's office, which he called the museum. The old-fashioned, wood and marble chair with marble worktables was the first rotary-drill chair brought to Europe from the U.S. His father had done his dental training at Harvard, Herr Tchumi told me proudly.

Alone with Herr Tchumi, I was losing some of the cockiness I'd felt after the speech. After all, if it hadn't been for this man and his quick action, filling me up with wine, I wouldn't have made it through. I offered to buy him a beer before I had to catch the train, and I remember trying to sound jovial, telling him that I owed him a drink after the wine at lunch; but, really, I felt ashamed now about what had happened.

He said no thanks to the beer; he had some work to do. So we said goodbye, and I started for the station. I didn't like it that my good spirits from after the speech were wearing off, so I stopped in a small restaurant and had a beer. Look, I had something to celebrate, didn't I? I had made it through the speech, hadn't I? I hadn't fallen apart; I wasn't gibbering away in a straitjacket, slobber drooling down my chin, was I? No. I had finished the speech, done all right, even done well, with a little help from Herr Tchumi and the wine.

But then it hit me: I would soon have to make another speech. What if they didn't serve wine? What if no Herr Rossler came through at the critical moment? Today didn't prove anything; after all, I had used all the tricks to get me through: the drops, the slides, the wine. Until I did it without all the tricks and props, I wouldn't have really done it. And though I can still see a certain truth in this kind of reasoning, what I'm more impressed with is how determined I was to see myself as a failure. It didn't matter that I had gotten through the speech. What mattered was that I hadn't gotten through it in the best way imaginable, and anything short of that was simply failure.

The rest of the speeches followed essentially the same pattern: first, several weeks of bone-wrenching dread and horrifying fantasies of failure; then the lonely train rides and someone meeting me at a station and taking me on a short tour of some local spot of interest (Roman Ruins or Medieval Castles); and, finally, the lunch itself, and wine, wine, wine, do your stuff.

And then afterwards, the self-accusations, the feelings of failure and guilt from drinking.

Once, I had two speeches back to back–one, a dinner meeting at Murten, and a luncheon the next day in Klein Basel. The president of the Murten Club, Herr Joseph Jeger, met me a the Murten station that afternoon and right away took me to a small restaurant where we had a beer. The waitress, a tall, curvy blond in her mid-thirties, knew Herr Jeger, and she smiled when he flirted with her. This guy was all right! Beer and women, and me not ten minutes off the train. What a relief, not to have to worry whether there would be wine at the meeting, because for once, I was going in with a full load from the start, and I'd gotten it legitimately, with the president of the club!

After a couple of beers, Herr Jeger asked me if I'd like to see some of the sights around Murten, and I said I would; so, he took me to the Roman ruins of the city of Aventicum AND to the medieval fortifications of the old walled town of Murten.

They did serve wine that night at the Rotary dinner, and I did drink it. After the speech, I went with Herr Jeger and a few of the members downstairs to the bowling alley in the basement of the restaurant, and we drank more wine there. Then, Herr Jeger was so enthusiastic about the speech, that when we got to his home, where I was staying for the night, he asked me to give it again for his pretty young wife. He dragged out his slide projector and screen, and uncorked a couple of bottles of white wine that the three of us drank while I showed the slides.

Of course, I paid for drinking all that wine with a fierce hangover, but there was no hiding out in my fourth-story room at the Rosslers. I had to take the train back to Basel and make another speech, this one at the Klein Basel Club, across the Rhein.

Frau Jeger took me to the train, and the next thing I remember is sitting in the restaurant of the Basel station, at a table near the door, slowly drinking red wine while I pretended to read a German newspaper. A half-liter bottle stood on the white cloth of the table, and when I had emptied it, I left the station with my airline bag.

I had decided to walk to Klein Basel, instead of taking the tram, so I could get some fresh air. Now, instead of worrying about the fear, I was afraid that I'd be too drunk to speak clearly. I remember walking down one of the curving, cobblestone streets toward the river and then crossing one of the newer bridges over the Rhein. By then, I felt almost happy in a giggly sort of way. I was feeling more fatigue than dread, and it seemed to me I had a secret from all the busy Baslers I saw hustling through the streets: here I was right in the middle of all these serious, industrious people, before noon on a working day, and I had a bottle of wine sloshing through my veins!

I can see another glass of wine at my place on the long table where I sat at the Rotary luncheon, and I still hear the small worry in my mind that I might slur the words of the speech.

Everything turned out fine, though, because Deiter Burkhardt of the Gross Basel Club told me after the speech that he had been at the Gross Basel meeting when I gave the speech there, but oddly enough, he had enjoyed it more this time. Somehow, it had seemed to have more fire. I smiled again at my little secret, but I didn't smile for long.

The next day, a day I *did* spend in the safety of my fourth-floor room, it came home to me just how bad things had gotten. Think of what I had done–drunk wine in order to get out from under the effects of drinking wine!

Now, everyone knows the seven danger signals of alcoholism. Or is it the seven danger signals of cancer, and the ten signs of alcoholism, or twelve, or anyway, you know those questions you ask yourself, answering *yes* to any *one* of which qualifies you as an alcoholic? Well, one of them goes something like, "Have you ever drunk to get over the bad effects of drinking?"

"*Yes!* I had!" was my answer, "And how! With a capital *Y!*"

And so, now, not only was I a freak who scared himself shitless over absolutely nothing, not only was I a coward who couldn't face the fear but had to hide behind every trick in the book to get through it, not only was I convinced that I had failed to meet the challenge of the speeches (even though I had given all six), but now...now I had to accept the fact that I was an alcoholic, a throwaway. And so, I pounded one more nail into the coffin that contained my future.

* * *

9

Today, I'm sitting out in the back yard, writing at my picnic table in the sun. Sound nice? Well, have a look around. An old gray cedar plank fence surrounds the small square of bare sandy earth on three sides, and the house completes the square. The paint of the house is peeling, and gray lines sprout up the walls–old tracks left behind when some past tenant pulled off the ivy that some tenant further past had cultivated.

The bare earth would be knee-high in leafy, wild plants and dry foxtails, but Ellie gets out now and roots them up. I used to sit in them before Ellie was here, before I made the table. Just sit in a low, aluminum beach chair, reading and watching derelict metal objects decay with salt rust in the ocean air: a ten-speed bike that used to be my only transportation, a dead water heater that was here when I came, and several long lengths of rust-flaking, steel pipe.

One friend who came by and saw me out here christened this place, "The Dog Yard," and I liked the name so much, I thought of using it in the title of a collection of short stories I never wrote: *Life in the Dog Yard*. Most of that has changed now that Ellie's here. The bicycle's gone, along with the water heater and pipes, and the weeds have been replaced by vine geraniums and nasturtiums. And here I am writing.

But there was one good thing then that's been changed for the worse--it used to be quiet here. Al, the retired Mexican-American who lived next door with his little dog, Killer, moved into a new condo on the hill above the railroad station. A gray-haired French lady owns the condo, and after several months of dating Al, she came one day and took him away in a powder-blue Cadillac; yes, she took Killer, too.

In the shack on the other side of us, old Mrs. Clark kept a quiet house alone. We were all proud of the way she could get along on her own at the age of eighty-six. She was a slender little lady who would always speak to us when she was sweeping off her front porch, and often she'd apologize for playing her radio late at night, but I never heard it once. I did hear her talking to herself, though, and one rainy winter night she came out on her porch and said to no one in particular, "I need some advice."

When she said it again, Ellie said, "She's talking to *us*," and I stepped out onto the porch to see what she wanted. She came over to her porch railing, and leaning toward me, she said quietly, "Some Mexicans followed me home from the market, and now they won't leave."

"Just wait right there," I said. "I'll get my shoes on and be right over." I hurried in and pulled on my shoes, telling Ellie to stand by at the phone. If she heard me yell, call the sheriff.

Walking out into the dark, I was all tensed up for something weird, and as I climbed the steps of Mrs. Clark's house, I pictured the dark, rough, illegal aliens who would meet me when I stepped into the lighted doorway. But when I did, I looked into an empty room. Mrs. Clark followed me in and exclaimed, "Why, where did they go?"

I quickly searched the bedroom and bathroom, and then went through her kitchen to the back door. It was hooked from the inside, so I knew no one had gotten out that way, unless of course, in her own neat way, Mrs. Clark had already hooked it behind them after they left.

When I stepped back into the small front room, Mrs. Clark stood under the light from a naked bulb in the ceiling socket. "They were right here," she said. "The little lady sat in this chair." She stepped toward a wing-backed chair that had a stack of blankets and a pillow on it. She snatched the pillow off the blankets, and I started back, expecting to see a tiny Mexican woman, but there was nothing but the blankets.

"Where did she go?" Mrs. Clark said, looking up at me.

"I don't know," I said.

"The man was sitting over there," she said, pointing to a straight-backed dining chair In front of a desk with a fold-out writing shelf. The shelf and the chair were covered with papers and envelopes, and the papers on the chair were smooth and unwrinkled. No one could have been sitting on them.

"I told them this was a one-person apartment," she said. "I hated to send them out in the rain, especially the little lady, but I just didn't have room for them. They wouldn't leave, so I just started fixing my dinner."

Of course, by then I knew she'd been hallucinating, or having visitors only she could see, and only when no one else was there.

"Look," I said, "I'll write down my phone number for you. If they come back, just call me. My name is Wallace, and my wife's name is Ellie. Just yell for us, if you need to."

"Oh, I know your names," she said.

She didn't call for us, but her lights stayed on all night long, and we could hear the sound of her low-heeled shoes tapping through the house, and from time to time, her soft-toned voice almost singing, "Little lady, oh, little lady, where are you?"

The next morning, her daughter and son-in-law came to get her. Though I didn't see them, Ellie told me when I got home from work that they'd taken Mrs. Clark away, and that all she'd carried with her was a pink electric blanket and a worried look.

Except for her last night here, Mrs. Clark was always quiet, but the neighbors we have now are growing a poisonous garden of sound around us.

Today, it's especially bad with the scuffle and whine of motorized hobby wood projects on one side, and the elastic screeching of a file on wood, back-and-forth, back-and-forth, coming from the other back yard; and from both, the falsetto wailing of male rock n' roll voices--just now as I write, it's Neil Young's nasal, whining search for a heart of gold.

Why don't I say anything to them? I can't. Can't face the greater pain of a confrontation. I look over at Ellie, sitting in the sunniest corner of the Dog Yard, wearing only a bikini. Her large, swelling stomach grows out forward more and more every day, looking like the front end of the California Zephyr, with the smooth button where her navel used to be, a single headlight.

It's a beautiful sight, but not a turn-on; an oblong, golden-brown watermelon that she takes out in the sun every day to ripen.

It seems strange that I'm not really fearing the coming, and it's getting awfully close. We go to Lamaze classes on Wednesday nights, and sure, I wonder how I'll do when I have to coach her through labor. But I'm trying not to think about that too much. Maybe it's this book. I do feel an inner pressure to get it finished before the baby comes, but that makes sense. I'm going to be too busy around here taking care of a new mother and baby to give any time to this long-play record of my own brand of poisonous whining. But maybe the writing helps me keep my mind off the future.

So, I've got to get on with it, noise or no noise. When I left off, I was pounding another nail into the coffin of my future, but as I look back now on that year, I can see that my future didn't die an easy death. As much as I felt I had reached a dead end, as much as I thought all the roads leading anywhere were blocked, I kept on acting like a man on his way someplace. My plan before all the catastrophes began falling across my path had been to go back to the States and continue graduate study in comparative literature. So, in the same way I'd gone through the motions of loading the slide projector at Olten, even though I didn't expect to be able to make the speech, I applied to graduate schools, even though I didn't feel I'd be able to function once I got into one.

What a macabre joke, filling out those forms. Each one had a section for stating why you intended to go into comparative literature as a profession. Intent! I know that a lot of shit gets shot in that section even by normal, idealistic, healthy, well-motivated college students, but by me? It was like a reporter asking a condemned man on the eve of his execution, "What would you do if someone gave you a million dollars?" I mean, the guy has the chair to think about, the rope, the bullet, and then? And then a blank, an unanswered question, or at best, a strong hope, so leave off with this fluff, this shit of a million dollars. But I went ahead and answered the questions, intent or no intent. If I only had a copy of one now. If I could read the carefully reasoned statements of how my study of comparative literature at their institution would improve the state of the world, Jesus, how I would howl.

All three of the schools I applied to required a proficiency in two foreign languages upon entrance, so I decided to brush up on the Russian I had learned my first two years in college. I enrolled in a beginning Russian course at the university.

It was a large class for first-year students, and I always sat in the back to keep all those eyes off the back of my neck. But one day I got there late, and only one seat remained at the far left end of a row near the front. front far-left row near the front. The teacher was working on a pronunciation exercise from the book, requiring each student to recite a group of five words containing the same sound. I turned to the page with the words and felt my heart begin to beat faster. Oh, no! It was happening to me here in class, even when I didn't have to stand up in front of everyone!

The teacher called on students in methodic order through the rows, and when she got to mine, I counted quickly ahead in the list in the book to see which group of words I'd have to pronounce. When I was sure I had the right ones, I rehearsed them silently under my breath. My head was beginning to tremble on my neck, so I cupped my chin in my right hand and leaned my elbow on the desk for support. Since I was sitting on the outside row of desks, there was no one to my left, and by opening my hand up the right side of my face and resting the edge of my jaw along my thumb, I could block out my view of the students to my right.

When my turn came, I could barely control my speech, but I managed to grind out the five words without the teacher making me pronounce any of them over again. When the hour was over, I stumbled from the class, knowing I wouldn't come back, watching my last hopes of graduate school die; and yet, in the coming weeks, I *still* acted as if they were alive.

I had already registered to take the Graduate Record Exam in Geneva, and I went ahead with my plans to take it. But now, I was afraid I'd panic during the test and not be able to finish it. Maybe I'd even suffer the final break.

But from what you've already read, can you perhaps guess that I made it through all right? In fact, I did quite well–well enough to help me get accepted by two of the three schools I applied to.

And then, after the GRE, after the letters of acceptance from the schools, what came next were the goodbyes. First, the formal goodbyes at the Rotary dinner at the famous Basel Zoological Gardens. The director was a Rotarian, and he took the members of the club and their families on a tour. I can remember walking along winding paths under the trees in the dreamy sunlight of a late summer dusk, and after dinner, shaking hands (with a dreamy load of wine in me) with the prudent members of the Basel business community while I received their good wishes for the future.

Then the personal goodbyes with Max and Jurg and Heiner and the band, and with Rosemarie, just home from school, and finally with Frau and Herr Rossler, standing on their front steps waving as Heiner drove me down the hill to take me to the station.

And then began the bleak hellos. The first from a pay phone in Kennedy Airport, a call home. By then, I was so afraid of what might happen to me in public, I wasn't sure I could operate the pay phone, and I had to stand and stare at it and wait for the veil of fear to lift that had fallen between my eyes and the slot for the coin.

Then came Baton Rouge and the questions of what I planned to do next with my life. I let them go by until one day, sitting on the small covered back patio of my parents' home drinking a beer with my father, he said, "The way I look at it, you can do anything you want." And I finally told him that I hardly felt able anymore to do the few things I *had* to do, much less anything I wanted. And then they both gave me what I needed, which was time and a place to let it slide along.

What I *had* to do was give more Rotary speeches. I came prepared with slides from Switzerland, and I finally took Frau von Eckhart's advice and got our family doctor to prescribe tranquilizers for the stage fright. Luckily, the Louisiana Rotary members weren't as hot to hear about Switzerland as the Swiss were to hear about Louisiana, and I was only invited to speak at three clubs.

130

After that ordeal was over, I let a lot of time slide while I sat and read on the back patio and watched the leaves on the trees change from green to mixed red and yellow, to brown and then bare branches. After a couple of fantasies of wandering around a strange New England campus alone, trying to register, I let that farce slide by, too.

Why, I ask myself now, why didn't I go see a shrink? Why did I think everything was over? If I'd had one of the seven danger signals of cancer, I would have run right down to the hospital and demanded a check-up and a cure. Why did I feel that everything was hopeless, and no efforts would be worth the trouble? Well, that was the problem. Part of the condition was hopelessness, and another part was the refusal to admit the condition. That's one of the craziest things about craziness—you can't admit being crazy.

Sometime in late fall, I came to feel I had to do something, anything to get me out of the dead end and out of my parents' house, so I drove downtown to the office of the Air Force recruiter. I had talked to him on the phone about getting into something that would use my language ability, and he had suggested Air Force Intelligence. Why? Why the military? I don't know. I couldn't stomach the idea of school or a regular job or just vegetating at my parents', and I wasn't brave or desperate enough to hit the road and see what would happen. So, the military.

And then, after I'd talked to an Air Force first sergeant and gotten several brochures, I stepped out into the hallway and met the next twist of my fate in the form of a short gunnery sergeant from the Marine Corps. He was leaning against the door frame of an office down the hall, and when I glanced at him, he nodded and said casually, "Say, sir, have you thought about giving *us* a try?"

The Marines? Me? At the point where I was afraid to tie my shoelaces in public, this casual little tough-guy was inviting *me* to become a gun slinger, a hired killer to do ol' Lyndon Johnson's dirty work in Vietnam? The *Marines*?

Well…well…. Why not? The *Marines*! Why hadn't I thought of it before? America's Foreign Legion. What a great, romantic way to end it all, in a war. Then, Gin would be sorry; everyone would be sorry, whoever "everyone" was. And sorry for what? I couldn't have formulated that in rational thought at that time.

I walked into the Gunny's office, and he called the officer selection officer in New Orleans. Very quickly I came to believe they had what I needed. Either they'd provide me with the definitive breaking point in training, or, if I made it through and on to the war, they'd provide ample opportunities for an honorable death. Of course, I didn't think it all out like that, especially not in such asinine terms as "honorable death." These are the words I can think of now to describe the goofy, nutty logic that I felt then only as a quick movement in the diaphragm.

And there was something else, too (and something else, and something else again, I'm sure, but this is what I could see at the time).

Somehow, if I did make it through the war without dying, but having offered myself up to it, then I could live again. I would have paid some kind of dues by risking death, and I could come back and say, "Screw you, Jack. I've done my time, and now I don't have to sweat the small stuff." Such was my crazy reasoning; and what's even crazier, it sort of worked that way.

* * *

10

The nurse who teaches our Lamaze class told us a story about a man who ran into the emergency room early one morning, yelling to the nurses to get outside and help his wife–she was having the baby right then in the backseat of their car! They rushed out behind him, but when they reached the car, it was empty. The man had left his wife at home, while he drove all the way to the hospital alone, keeping up some kind of hallucinatory drama with an empty back seat. The nurses sent an ambulance to pick up the real wife.

As our nurse told the story, I laughed along with the rest of the expectant mothers and fathers, but I have to admit, I felt a small flutter of fear in my stomach.

Just think, that really happened to someone! Some poor man now lives with that story and its retelling; lives with the fact that something in his psyche can produce a stronger reality than the one that actually exists in a ten-foot radius around his body.

And of course, I wondered if it could happen to me.

But it turned out that Ellie's labor was real enough. It started about three-thirty in the morning, but she didn't wake me until six, shaking me gently by the shoulder.

"I think I'm in labor," she said quietly.

"Good," I said. "Good." But I was thinking, *Oh-shit-oh-shit-oh-shit, it's here!* "What does it feel like?" I said. "Are you hurting?"

"Not really. Just little twinges. It might be false labor."

"Let's get ready, anyway." I was trying to sound confident and businesslike, like someone she could depend on. I rolled out of bed and headed into the kitchen. All I had to do was fix my own breakfast and a sandwich to take to the hospital. Ellie's bag was sitting by the front door, she had packed it and stationed it there two weeks before, when our doctor said the baby could come any minute.

And for two weeks, we went to bed every night, fully expecting that it would. Standing at the stove, I broke an egg in the skillet and stuck a piece of bread in the broiler. Then I walked to the back door and opened it and looked out.

There were streaks of fleecy clouds lit pink by the coming sunrise against a dark blue sky. Directly overhead, there was an exact half-moon, and I mumbled, "Help us now, Moon. Help us, Wakan Tanka, that our people may live."

"Hey, Wallace," Ellie called from the bathroom, "I think my water just broke."

"Is there a lot?"

"No, hardly any."

"Don't you think you ought to call the doctor?"

"I'd hate to wake him up for false labor."

"*Jesus,* call him! He gets *paid* to be waked up for false labor." I was getting jumpy now. I didn't feel like eating, but the nurse at Lamaze class said to make sure to eat if I had time. Coaching labor takes a lot of energy.

While I ate, Ellie called the doctor, and he told her to come on in and he'd meet us at the hospital. When I finished eating, Ellie was ready to go. I took her bag out and put it in the back seat of her VW, and then carried out the box with the infant seat and put it in the trunk. Ellie came down the steps, and when she looked at me, we both laughed.

"Oh my God, I hope it's not false labor," she said.

"Look, it doesn't matter if it is. It doesn't *matter*."

I pulled off, driving slowly over the bumps and potholes in our dirt road, and I reminded myself to drive slowly all the way. I thought of the man who'd left his wife, and I looked at Ellie to make sure she was real.

"Drive a little faster," she said. "It's starting to hurt."

"Do you want to start the breathing?" I said, thinking, *Oh shit, it really is here.*

"No. I just want to get there."

We drove up Torrey Pines Hill, and now the sun was above the mountains to the east. We passed the famous Torrey Pines Golf Course and then turned on the road toward the hospital, the sun now hitting us full in the face.

"Well, it's a beautiful day," I said.

"Yes," Ellie said.

At the hospital, we in the front door, and the woman at the reception desk came out before we said anything and pulled a wheelchair from a line of them near the elevator.

"Do I have to sit in that?" Ellie said.

"You sure do," the woman said, smiling.

Ellie sat down in the chair, and I pushed it onto the elevator. When the doors shut, Ellie said she felt silly sitting in a wheelchair.

"It'll just be for a second," I said, but I was already in the labor room, rehearsing what I was supposed to be doing during Ellie's contractions: timing her breathing to relax her muscles, describing images and positive thoughts to take her mind off the pain, massaging the small of her back.

A nurse met us at the elevator and took us to a labor room and left us while Ellie changed into a hospital gown. When the nurse came back, she brought Ellie a cup of apple juice, and she asked me if I would like anything to eat.

"No thanks," I said, "I've had breakfast."

"Breakfast," she said. "You had time for breakfast?" Then looking at Ellie, she said, "And I guess *you* had to fix it for him."

"No," Ellie said, "He fixes his own breakfast."

I remember wondering if this was the way they built up your confidence for labor. Was this the way they were smoothing a man's entry into the traditionally female world of birth? I felt like a little boy whose mother had just defended him from another critical mother.

And if that wasn't unsettling enough, another nurse came in to measure the baby's heartbeat with an electronic stethoscope. It looked like a black cassette recorder with a chrome disk dangling from it on the end of a heavy rubber wire. The nurse squirted some cream on the disk and turned on the amplifier box, then placed the disk against Ellie's bare stomach. Static came over the box, but no heartbeat. The nurse moved the disk around from one spot to another without getting any heartbeat sound from the amplifier, and I noticed her hands were trembling.

"I'm sorry," she said, "I guess this thing's not working." She left, and I fought back an inclination to get reassurance from Ellie.

"It's okay," I said. "It's just that the thing doesn't work."

Just then, another nurse walked in, a tan young woman with long, blond hair pulled severely back and caught with a tortoise-shell clip at the nape of her neck. She carried a low-tech obstetrical stethoscope with a horn between the ear tubes, and she quickly put it on and pressed the horn against Ellie's stomach.

"His heartbeat sounds good and strong," she said. "About one-hundred-twenty beats a minute. Just right."

She told us she had just come on shift and she'd be our nurse for the next eight hours, if the labor lasted that long. After the experience with the first two nurses, I felt lucky at the shift change.

We turned out to have a lucky shift change in doctors, too. The one we called that morning was just one of four in the clinic we went to, and they split the deliveries between them in shifts. This one made me nervous from the start, because he was nervous that we wouldn't let him use the fetal monitor. It's a machine that looks like the one an auto mechanic hooks up to your car when he's tuning it, with similar knobs and lights and dials. They use it to monitor the baby's condition during labor, but we didn't want it because of the way it has to be attached.

They can either fasten a belt around the mother's stomach, but Ellie didn't want that because then she couldn't get up and walk; or they can attach wires to the baby in the uterus, by sticking a metal clip into the baby's scalp, essentially, a staple through the skin.

Now, I can hear the hard-nosed, brass-tacks types muttering, "Oh, God, save us from the bleeding heart routine. It doesn't hurt the baby."

Maybe not, but I'd like to invite anyone who believes that to step up close to where I'm sitting at my writing desk. That's right, step over and bend your head down. I've got a very small stapler that we can test your theory with. And if it hurts that aging scalp of yours, so proudly toughened in the school of hard knocks, what would it do to the tender, palpitating scalp of an infant who's been soaking in warm water for nine months?

Another thing I didn't like about this doctor was the way he kept trying to hurry the process. It turned out that Ellie's water hadn't broken, after all, so the doctor was going to reach in with one of the long, plastic sticks with a tiny hook on one end that they use to snag a hole in the amniotic sac.

Just as he bent over to shove that evil plastic snag into her, the clear fluid came flowing out, and I saw him flinch backwards. He looked up at me and said, "It broke. The water broke." And I noticed that he was swallowing back his nausea.

And then, after only two hours of labor, the doctor said if Ellie didn't start dilating faster, he'd have to do a Caesarean section.

Now, all during Ellie's pregnancy, and even when before the pregnancy, when we were in the planning stages of having a baby, we thought only of a natural childbirth—no drugs and no knives allowed. So, you can imagine the effect it had on us to hear this pronouncement only two hours into labor. One effect you may not have imagined was that Ellie started to dilate.

She helped herself, though, by insisting on getting up and walking in between contractions. I remember seeing single drops of blood spaced along the tile floor as we walked back and forth, and one of those spots is still in the knee of my light-brown corduroys from when I knelt beside the bed, massaging the small of Ellie's back.

After the doctor was satisfied that Ellie had started to dilate, he left us mostly alone until the end of his shift, and we did the things I had rehearsed on the elevator: breathing through each contraction, imaging walks in the mountains, and walking between contractions.

When Ellie's cervix had dilated to ten centimeters, the doctor who had come on duty told her she could start pushing. This was it. Now she had to help the contractions push the baby down the short distance of the birth canal. But that short distance can be impossibly long, and after two hours of Ellie's pulling her knees up to her chest at the start of each contraction, panting, blowing, grunting the baby down further, the doctor came in and said she'd have to stop.

"But I could keep this up all day," Ellie said.

"Yes, *you* could, but the baby couldn't. The pushing is dangerous for its brain." He gave us twenty minutes more, and when the baby still hadn't moved any further down, he said he was going to do a low forceps delivery.

That was better than a C-section, but not much. Have you ever seen forceps? Have you ever seen a pair of those steel, scissor-handled tongs some people keep in their kitchen to lift hot potatoes out of boiling water? Well, imagine a big pair, chrome plated, big enough to fit around a baby's head and jerk it out of the womb, whether it wants to come or not. And that's what they were going to use to jerk *our* baby out. Before they did, they'd give Ellie a shot in the spine to deaden her from the waist down, and that drug would be in the baby's bloodstream within a matter of seconds, depressing its ability to breathe once it was out.

Once the doctors took over, things moved fast. They brought in a table and transferred Ellie from her table in our little room to a wheeled gurney and sped her off to the surgical delivery room.

In a small prep room, the nurse gave me a green surgical suit and cap to wear. Then I had to wait in the hall while the anesthesiologist did his work, and they let me into the bright room.

I stood at the head of the table, holding Ellie's hands and watching those busy people work. Two nurses strapped Ellie's numb legs into the raised metal stirrups, and the doctor placed a large upright mirror behind him at the foot of the table, so we could see the birth.

Now in the mirror, I could see the top of the baby's head, a circle of scalp pressing the lips of the vagina open. The skin was dark gray, almost blue. *Too dark. Oh, my God, too dark*!

The doctor slipped the large steel clamps in around the head, and I flinched inwardly at the sight of the steel pressing against flesh, but Ellie was looking up at me and didn't even feel what had happened. One of the nurses stood on one side of Ellie, and the anesthesiologist stood on the other, and when the doctor began to pull, they pushed on the baby through Ellie's stomach.

Ellie slipped downward on the table, and I said, "Do you want me to hold her?"

"I don't think that will be necessary," the doctor said. In the mirror, I could see him sitting on a short stool, levering down with the forceps, pushing against the edge of the table as a fulcrum. Ellie began to slide, and I slipped my arms under her armpits and pulled her back up.

"I guess you better hold her," the doctor said. "This is a big baby."

Slowly, slowly, he pulled, and the others pushed, and I leaned back to keep Ellie from sliding down the table. And slowly the head came out in the chrome steel clamps, and the whole head was the dark color of the scalp.

Everyone was tight-lipped with the strain, but when the head was out, the doctor said to Ellie, "Look, the head's out," but she didn't look, and the doctor said again, "*Look*, the head's out."

Ellie raised her head and looked in the mirror and then dropped back and said to me, "Poor baby, poor baby," crying quietly.

"It's got big shoulders," the doctor said, starting to pull again, turning the head now, twisting it with the steel clamps to get the shoulders to turn.

"*They're ruining it*," I thought. "*They're ruining it*."

140

Then the shoulders came, and the doctor stood up and took the baby under the armpits as it slooped out the rest of the way. He drew it up in his arms, and in the middle of all that strain, I remember a calm thought in the back of my mind about the umbilical cord. It didn't look like I expected, but like a braided length of blue and pink intestine.

"It's a boy!" a female voice shouted, and the doctor balanced the small, wet body on one arm, while he clamped and (*don't!*) snipped the still-pulsing cord. They rushed him over to a plastic tray with a heating lamp over it and cupped a small black mask over his face.

He's not crying!

When they put him in the tray, my view was blocked by a machine that the mask was connected to by a black hose. All I could see was a small white leg.

He's not crying!

"Is he dead?" Ellie asked, her face broken with crying.

"No," I said, "He's not dead."

He's dead. He is dead and we've lost him, and everything is tumbling down, all the hopes, the careful planning. But at least we have each other. I leaned down and cradled Ellie's wet face against mine, and I felt a quick feeling of consolation, like crawling alone at night into a strange bed in the dark of a strange hotel room in a strange city, thinking that at least there's sleep to hide in.

A muffled sob–*it's him! He's crying!* They pulled the mask off and let the yells out into the room. *He's alive!* The pain of new tears flows over my eyes. *He's alive!*

They brought him over and put him on Ellie's bare breasts, and he stopped crying. He opened his eyes, but then shut them against the bright lights. Then someone said we had to move again, to a recovery room. They wanted to take him back and put him in the warming pan for the ride, but Ellie said no, she wanted *me* to carry him.

One of the nurses put a small blanket over him and helped me pick him up. I cradled him against my heart and walked carefully down the hall, following the nurse. In the recovery room, I asked the nurse to turn off all the lights. The light coming in through the windows to the nurses' station was enough.

I sat down on a chair and waited for them to wheel Ellie in. As I sat looking at his face, he opened his eyes again and looked quietly back at me.

"Max, you're Max," I whispered, the whisper breaking. "We're going to call you Max."

And that's what we've called him now for three weeks. And it's strange, but now that I'm sitting here writing this with Max and Ellie asleep in the bedroom, it occurs to me that I went through all that without my usual fear of freaking. I guess I was too busy to think once things got started, but there seems to be something else as well, something deeper that has nothing at all to do with the person I usually think of as Wallace, and all his fears and worries and misgivings.

It's as though I found out that I've been living something that's more than that. All this time, I've been living the life of a human, and I didn't even know it. All this time, I thought I was living this small, freaked-out, lonely individual life, and then all of a sudden, I'm faced with something that repeats itself over and over again—childhood and parenthood, always returning.

And sometimes at night, when I bend over his bed and listen to his small breaths in the dark, I get a flash of one of my parents bending over my bed in the dark years ago, and that's when the feeling is strongest. Then, I'm no longer some alienated ant of the twentieth century, but the next-to-last link in a long chain of being;

and then for a moment I'm free of my tiny, self-centered circling, and I feel I'm on some large circle of life that's beginning a new revolution with this new child, Max.

* * *

11

Today, I'm at the library again, waiting for two guys at the table behind me to shut up so I can get started and bring this whining rehash of my painful year in Europe to a close. But they keep it right up. One just sat down, and he's shifting around, shuffling papers, snapping his ring binder, talking in a voice that could be heard in a boiler room, and now he's whistling! That's right, *whistling*. A tuneless whee-whoo-whoo-whee-whoo that I find hard to believe.

I turn around in my seat and look at him, and I notice that the girl at the next table is doing the same. He glances at me and stops whistling, and I turn back forward. But he keeps talking in the same loud voice to his friend about the homework, about the test they have next Monday, about the professor.

Should I get up and assert myself, or try to last it out till he settles down? Either way, I'm screwed. Either way, I'm getting all riled up. The longer I sit here, the more cowardly wretched I feel, but every time I think of getting up, my neck crawls with reluctance.

But finally, it's too much–I'm going to complain. But I'll keep it cool--assertive, but not aggressive. I'll try to keep from creating an adversary situation. I'll just tell the two of them that I can't concentrate when they're talking. They can't argue with *that*, can they? My heart's thumping now. I hope they don't see my hands tremble. All right, here goes.

I stood up and stepped back to the whistler and leaned down toward him, placing one hand on his table. His hair was short and carrot red, and he had a wispy, carrot-colored beard.

"When you talk like that," I whispered, "I can't concentrate on what I'm doing."

He glanced up at me and then looked straight ahead without answering.

He reached up and pulled at the beard and then said quickly, "After all, this is a library, and I don't see any signs around that say 'Quiet'. "

I couldn't digest that at first, so I just stood there leaning on my arm without saying anything. "After all, this is a library, and I don't see any signs around that say 'quiet'?" The little circuits inside my head were firing, but they couldn't fit the logic of that together. I should have been the one to say, "After all, this is a library." What could he possibly mean by it, that libraries are places where you go to *talk*, for Christ's sake?

No answer to that one came to me, and I stood over him thinking with mounting frustration that I'd probably have to go somewhere else to write, since this guy was going to insist on his right to talk and whistle, because *after all*, this *was* a *library*.

Then he pulled at the side of his beard with his fingertips and said, "Well, I guess we could go someplace else to study."

"I'd appreciate that," I said. And then, out of gratitude, I said in a placating tone, "You know, I'm not studying the same things you are, so what you say breaks my concentration."

But he didn't answer, so I straightened up and walked back to my table. As I sat down, I heard him say something to his friend, but the only words I caught were, "pissed off." Whether he was saying that he was pissed off or that I was, I didn't know. Now it was my turn to shuffle papers until I could calm down and get back to work.

I'm glad I did it, but at the same time, I felt like a Nazi. Is it just me? How do the other students in this building stand it? Is everyone else able to shut out the noise?

If so, then why do they come here to study? They could do just as well in their dorm rooms, couldn't they, with their roommates talking on the phone about who they buggered last night, or who buggered them?

But don't I have enough questions of my own to answer without asking any about the lives of these students, enough crap of my own to stir without stirring theirs? And you must be asking some questions, too, like, "Where is all this stirring getting us?"

Someplace, I think. In fact, for several years, I've seen a glimmer of an idea that I still had someplace to go. The first glimpse I got was just after I got out of the Marines, and I was lying alone on a California beach reading a back issue of *Psychology Today*. In that issue, there was an article about a group of doctors who were treating schizophrenia by not treating it, especially by not administering drugs. Their idea was that any so-called emotional imbalance was really an effort by the psyche to reestablish its own balance in its own way, and it shouldn't be stopped by drugging the patient out of contact with it.

I remember sitting up and looking around at the beach and the ocean, and feeling a little thrill run up my backbone. There were people out there who didn't think of me as a throwaway! In fact, they thought that what I was going through was a natural process, and that instead of needing to avoid anything or hide anything, I should be living through it more completely. Far from Mailer's idea that a break was a failure that simply led to deeper failures in the future, they seemed to be saying that the break was necessary, and a failure only from the perspective of the life before the break—that it was necessary before you could begin to put the pieces together to fit the new perspective.

"Getting enlightenment from a slick magazine on a California beach?" you smile snidely.

Yes, why not, if it works? I mean, if what the masters of enlightenment teach about the nature of God and things is true, then God is just as much God in a back issue of *Psychology Today* as God is God in a backcountry ashram in India. And if God is God in whatever guise, then you are still you in every act, and not simply a failure to have been something better.

And how about this? Did you know that at one point in Clark Gable's career, his hands shook when he was on camera? Yeah, how about that! Smooth Clark. And what did he do about it? Run off and join the Marines? No! Some young director suggested he should stick his hands in the pockets of his coat. Simply that—stick his hands in his jacket pockets. And listen to this: you know Lauren Bacall's trademark look, head cocked a bit, eyes slanting up at the camera? Well, she too had problems with trembling on camera, but instead of her hands, it was her neck, and she found that if she lowered her head a little, it eased the trembling.

So, they both used tricks. Does that mean they were failures? That, somehow, they didn't accomplish anything? That all their movies should be burned? No, it just means that they coped with being what they were, instead of tossing themselves on the dung heap because they couldn't fit an image of something better.

Don't worry, though. This isn't a call to unleash all the shaking crazies like me and Lauren Bacall and Clark Gable onto the world that so many steady folks are trying so hard to perfect.

Of course, I'm talking most pointedly to myself (as crazies are known to do), to my own perfectionist voice who tells me I'm not good enough.

Right now, it's saying, "Well, that's all right for Clark Gable and Lauren Bacall. But what if *you* not only trembled, what if *you* got so scared *you* couldn't even talk? What if your hands shook so bad, you couldn't even hit a nail with a hammer?"

All right, Dammit! What if? But I have to go do it. I have to complete it. I can't make a life of *what ifs*! At least then I'll have something real to deal with, and not be living a *what if* existence, always running away from something that *might* have happened.

"Well, great!" I can hear you saying. "What a lesson he's teaching. If I have emotional problems, all I have to do is just let go and freak out and join the Marines and get shipped off to war, and everything will be fine. That, and get married and have a baby and bang! I'll be tied in with the movement of the cosmos. Is that the moral of this story?"

And I say, *That's it*! That's what you do if you just happened to be me in the year after I graduated from college, and then you studied for a year in Europe and started having panic attacks, and when you reached the dead end, you joined the Marines and shipped out to Vietnam, and came back and learned cabinet making, and went back to college, and decided to write a book.

But if you happen to be someone else, then you've got to work it out however it wants to be worked out for you.

And if that's not lesson enough for you, if you still want a stronger moral for the story, well, *here's* a moral for you:

On a cold morning in March, 1868, Friedrich Nietzsche went out to perform his duties as a volunteer in the Fourth Prussian Horse Artillery at Naumburg, a garrison town in Prussia. When he tried to mount his horse, Balduin ("one of the most restive and fiery animals in the battery," according to Nietzsche's sister), the horse bucked and threw Nietzsche, wounding him in the chest with a blow from the pommel.

Even though he was seriously hurt, Nietzsche kept trying to mount the horse until he succeeded. Then, he completed the riding exercise in terrible pain from the wound.

For two days, Nietzsche suffered on in silence, and then fainted while on duty. By now, the torn muscles in his chest were infected, and it took five months of convalescence and treatment by the famous surgeon, Volkmann of Halle, before the wound healed. It was serious enough to terminate Nietzsche's military service, and he carried a large scar on his chest for the rest of his life.

Twenty-one years later, on January the third, 1889, during another cold winter morning, , Friedrich Wilhelm Nietzsche left his rented room in in Turino, Italy, and stepped out for a walk on the Piazza Carlo Alberto. There on the square, he saw a coachman beating a horse. Bursting into tears, Nietzsche ran to the horse and threw his arms around its neck and hung there, sobbing. He had to be carried back to his room, and it turned out that the encounter had precipitated a nervous collapse, one that had recently been building. The diagnosis was progressive paralysis, probably brought on by syphilis.

This final break came when Nietzsche was forty-five years old. He lived for eleven more years, first in his mother's care, then after her death in 1897, in his sister's, paralyzed in his right side, sometimes lucid, most often not.

As I think back now, it seems to me that I too tried to mount a difficult horse the cold morning I couldn't get a spoon of ice cream to my mouth, and I carried the wound ever since, even though I was the only one who knew it was there.

Now, in comparing myself to Nietzsche, I'm aware that he was an earthshaking thinker, while I was a hand-shaking drinker, and after all, I didn't succeed in raising the spoon. Still, it was often the case that in the times when my heart pounded and my hands shook, it felt like I had mounted a horse I couldn't control. And as the horse galloped away with me, all I could do was grab a fistful of mane in each hand and hold on during the wild ride, doing my best to stay on the horse's back, and at the same time, not show anyone how God-awful scared I was.

After I read about Nietzsche's two significant experiences with horses, I labeled my experience, "Riding Nietzsche's Horse." And before each ride, whenever I was building up a case of stage fright, or anxiety attack, one of my worst fears was that my friends would find me sprawled on the ground with the horse, sobbing with my arms around its neck.

Overly dramatic? You bet! And I guess that helps me make something bigger out of what I've come to learn is a fairly run-of-the-mill anxiety disorder.

I've ridden Nietzsche's Horse across the sunny campuses of California colleges and into construction company offices, even into a restaurant where all I had to do was eat a meal with an old friend I hadn't seen for several years.

And what lessons did all those rides teach me? Eventually, I came to accept the reality that my fear of the ride was always worse than the ride itself, and that if I wanted to grow, I would need to face new situations that required me to ride.

I also found that I was riding all wrong. I was fighting too hard against the horse. I needed to learn to relax in the saddle and let the horse take me where I needed to go. To ease my grip on the mane and let myself go with the roll of the big horse's gallop, riding hard into the unknown, keeping a sharp lookout for pleasant surprises ahead.

And in a way, that's what I've done in this circling process that I've asked you to suffer through with me. It hasn't led to any earth shattering realizations or awakenings in my life, but it has allowed me to take one more step in creating a life I can live.

And even if that's it, nothing more than that, I'll take it.

* * *

Made in the USA
Columbia, SC
18 May 2024

35868624R10095